TENSE

VOLUME TWO

NEW YORK TIMES BESTSELLING AUTHOR

DEBORAH BLADON

FIRST ORIGINAL EDITION, MAY 2017

ISBN-13: 978-1546316749
ISBN-10: 1546316744
eBook ISBN: 9781926440446

Book & cover design by Wolf & Eagle Media

www.deborahbladon.com

Chapter 1

Sophia

"You look like hell," Cadence says as she slams my apartment door shut with her foot. "Take these from me, Soph. I think my hands fell asleep on the train."

I reach forward and grab the handles of the two large shopping bags that are clutched tightly in her fists. "You have to let go if you want me to take them."

She chuckles as she looks down at her hands. "Good point."

"Why did you bring so much food?" I ask even though I already know the answer to that question. When Cadence panics, she cooks. It's the only way she can calm herself down. Since she told me she was pregnant, I've repeatedly joked with her that once the contractions start, she'll be in the kitchen whipping up a four-course gourmet meal. She laughs it off, but I'm not convinced it won't happen.

She finally uncurls her hands to let me take the bags. "You didn't eat dinner. I'm going to cook that for you now and then I'll make something you can heat up for breakfast. You need all the energy you can get when you go see Mr. Foster to fight for your job in the morning."

I doubt like hell I'll have to fight for it. Nicholas told me two hours ago that Mr. Foster fired me, but I haven't heard a thing from my boss all night. If there's one constant about Gabriel Foster, it's that he's a reasonable man. I may have witnessed him fangirling all over Nicholas in the office the other day, but he's not the type to succumb to gossip.

Mr. Foster relies on cold, hard facts and in this case, there aren't any that support the accusations Nicholas was throwing at me. I even have the flash drive that he gave me with his book on it as proof. I found it in the clutch Dexie loaned me. That's where I put it after Nicholas handed it to me at his place and that's where it was tonight when I went looking for it after getting home from Hibiscus.

I didn't chase after Nicholas when he left the restaurant. I couldn't. I know that he wasn't open to listening to anything I would have said. Wasting my time trying to convince him that I didn't steal his manuscript would have been pointless. The mere fact that he thinks I'm capable of it pisses me off.

"I think Mr. Foster will see my side of things." I place both bags on the kitchen island. "He's always telling me that I'm the best assistant he's ever had. He's not going to fire me based on the crazy rantings of a man he barely knows."

"You don't think it matters that the man in question just so happens to be one of the most successful novelists on the planet?" She tugs a bunch of carrots and an eggplant from one of the bags. "Why would Nicholas tell you that you're fired if you're not?"

"Why would he say any of the things he said to me?" My tone is clipped. I explained every detail about what happened between Nicholas and me at Hibiscus to Cadence on the phone on my way home. I don't want to go there again. I've been struggling to keep it together since Nicholas walked away from me. Crying won't solve a thing, so I'm fighting back the urge to do it.

She eyes me suspiciously. "You're so damn calm, Soph. How can you be this together right now? Your boyfriend just got you fired, threatened you with a lawsuit and broke up with you. Nicholas Wolf messed up your entire life in the span of one night."

"I didn't do anything wrong, Den. Nicholas has no proof. I have the truth on my side. He can think whatever he wants about me, but I know that I'm innocent and there's no way he can prove otherwise."

"If you need a character witness to back you up when you go talk to Mr. Foster, I'll be there."

I reach for the one cutting board she left behind when she moved. "I can handle Gabriel. I'll march into his office in the morning and tell him exactly what happened. I'm innocent. The only thing I'm guilty of is dating a jerk."

***

"Mr. Foster?" I ask tentatively. He's in early, which rarely happens now. Before he met his wife, my boss always arrived at the office before me and each afternoon when I left for the day, he'd still be sitting behind his desk in the exact spot he is now. "Can I speak with you, sir?"

His head snaps up. He'd been staring at the screen of his laptop when I first got in twenty minutes ago. I took my time hanging up my coat before I turned on my computer, checked my emails and then finally got up to approach his open office door.

"Sophia?" His brow knits when his gaze meets mine. "I didn't expect to see you today."

Shit. Maybe Nicholas Wolf did convince Gabriel to kick my ass to the curb outside this luxurious office tower.

"Why not?" I ask bluntly. I came to the office with my emotional armor on and my battle plan in place. I won't leave this building without a fight.

He pushes both of his palms against the edge of his desk and rises from his chair. I watch in silence as he rounds the desk and moves to close his office door.

I swallow hard. Mr. Foster has only closed his door twice when we've been talking. The first was when he told me he was going to be a father. His eyes had welled with tears and his voice cracked. I knew that day he closed the door so no one would see his strong façade crumble. The other time was when I'd messed up on an email I drafted for him. There was no harm, since back then he always double checked the emails I'd send on his behalf. He was disappointed in me though and when the door closed, I could see it immediately in his expression. I don't see that now. There's something else simmering just below the surface.

"Please have a seat." He taps his fingers against the back of one of the two chairs that face his desk.

I hesitate briefly before I lower myself into it, taking special care to tuck the fabric of my skirt in place in my lap. I wore this particular outfit today because I always like to have a Plan B in case Plan A goes up in smoke. Today, my Plan B is to sell Mr. Foster on my designs if he fires me from my job as his assistant. This dress is one of my first creations and it fits the Arilia label to a tee. I may be delusional in thinking he'd even consider giving my work a place on a rack in his store, but I'll always wonder if I don't try.

"I emailed the manager of the Liore store in Paris just now." I tug on the end of a small loose thread on the left side seam of the skirt. "I sent her the inventory list for next month. She likes to plan her display window at least two weeks ahead of the products hitting the racks. I sent along my suggestions as I do each month."

He takes a step toward me but stills at my words. His gaze travels over my black skirt and red blouse. "I'm very impressed."

Mr. Foster doesn't do sarcasm, so I take the compliment as genuine. "Thank you, sir."

I'm biding my time, hoping that he'll remember each and every day I stayed late so he could rush home to his wife and daughter. I need him to keep in mind that I trekked through a blizzard less than six weeks ago when the city had virtually shut down under a blanket of two feet of snow. He was in Italy and needed me to find a file for him and I did it without hesitation even though all I wanted to do was stay in bed that cold, Saturday morning.

"Nicholas Wolf called me last night just as I was leaving the office." He sinks into the chair next to me. "He had a lot to say."

"So I heard," I begin as I cross my legs. "I met up with him after your conversation. He told me you two spoke. I'd like a chance to explain things to you before you fire me."

He shoots me a look that's a clear mix of surprise and sympathy. "You don't need to explain anything, Sophia. I've made up my mind."

"You've made up your mind? You did that without hearing my side?" I rub the bridge of my nose. "You can't fire me. I didn't do anything."

"Today is your last day working as my assistant."

I inhale sharply trying to catch my breath. I feel like I've been punched square in the stomach. "You can't do this. I didn't steal anything from him. He's wrong. I would never do that."

He straightens and leans back in the chair. "I believe you. I have no doubt that he's mistaken."

"Really?" I fist my hands together on my lap. "If you believe me, why are you firing me?"

"Where's your phone?" He glances toward the closed office door. "Did you leave it on your desk?"

Did he leave his mind at home? What the hell does it matter where my phone is right now? I'm in the middle of a career crisis. "I did. Why?"

"Did anyone call you this morning?"

My mom did. It's typical. The morning after she meets with her book club she calls me, usually before I start work to tell me if the book her club read is a thumbs-up or down. She knows I have a very mild interest in fiction. After last night, I doubt I'll read another book again. At the very least I'll steer clear of detective novels written by crazy hot men with trust issues.

"My mom," I confess because I'm confused as hell and just as tired. I barely slept. Instead, I fought the heartburn from the vinegar bathed salad Cadence served me before she whipped up the pasta dish. "She always calls me after her book club."

He smiles. "I was hoping you'd received a call from Sasha by now."

Sasha Berga.

She's the self-proclaimed Queen of the design department at Foster Enterprises. She skipped past retirement age more than a decade ago, but she's clinging to her job with both of her well-manicured hands. I've only shared one conversation with her and that was focused on Arilia's winter fashion line from a year ago. She asked my honest opinion about it while she was waiting for Mr. Foster to finish a meeting. I gave my unvarnished view of the mess that it was and she arched both brows, scowled and never said another word to me again.

"I haven't talked to Sasha." I have no desire to. The only person I want to talk to right now is sitting next to me. He already said that he didn't believe Nicholas so it makes zero sense for him to send my ass packing. I make a mental note to call Zoe Beck, the only attorney I know, to help me launch a lawsuit against Foster Enterprises for wrongful dismissal.

"You should, Sophia. I assumed you would spend the day with her."

Why the hell would I spend my day with a woman who took offense at my candid critique of the hideous items she personally chose for that collection last year? In her eyes, I'm akin to the dirt on the bottom of her Louboutins.

"I'd rather talk to you about my job. I need this job, Mr. Foster."

"No, you don't." He stands.

I beg to differ so I stand too. I rest my hands on my hips in a failed effort to look intimidating. "I do. I really need this job."

He reaches across his desk to pick up his laptop, turning the screen toward me. "You have a job. We're launching a new line for the fall. Our target audience is women your age who have a limited budget for fashion. There's a spot for you on the design team if you want it."

I gaze at his face briefly before I glance down at the computer. "That's my website. You've seen my website? How did you find it?"

"Nicholas told me you two were meeting Claudia Stefano for dinner last night. When I finally got a word in, I asked why and he told me she was considering selling some of your designs in her stores."

I quirk a brow. I've had it all wrong. Mr. Foster isn't firing me. He's giving me the opportunity of a lifetime. "You like my designs, sir?"

"I like them enough to start the hunt for a new executive assistant to replace you. You may be the most talented designer on staff. Sasha is waiting for you in her office. If you want the job, just say the word."

I don't. Instead, I let my actions speak for me as I dart out of his office and head straight for the elevator that will take me two floors down to the design department and my new boss, the one and only, Sasha Berga.

Chapter 2

Sophia

"I can't believe I'm the newest member of the Ella Kara design team." I park my elbows on my kitchen table and rest my chin in my palm.

"You're what?" Cadence takes a bite of a stalk of celery covered in chocolate syrup.

I swallow back the urge to vomit in my mouth. "Why do you have to eat things like that? What is it with pregnant women?"

"Pregnant women?" She asks dryly. "I'm the only pregnant woman you know."

"Incorrect." I slide a paper napkin from the pile I keep on the table toward her. "You have chocolate on your cheek."

"I don't need the napkin." Her fingers brush over her cheek, transforming the chocolate from a simple, circular sphere to a long elegant line. "Who else is pregnant? Jesus, Soph, tell me you're not having Nicholas Wolf's baby."

I laugh aloud. "That will never happen. I'm not the pregnant one. Gabriel's wife is. I found out today."

"Did you find this out before or after he fired you?"

I reach across the table to tap her forehead twice. "Try to follow along, Mama. I'll repeat word-for-word what I told you in the voicemail message I left you earlier. Mr. Foster gave me a job in the design department. I'm working on the new line that launches next fall. It's called Ella Kara. It's named after his daughter Ella and his baby-to-be, Kara, who is going to be about two months younger than your baby."

"Information overload." She dips the end of the celery back in the jar of syrup she found in the back of my refrigerator. "So Nicholas Wolf wasn't entirely wrong? Mr. Foster did fire you?"

I sigh. After I had spent three hours with Sasha, I went back up to Gabriel's office and as I packed up the personal items from my desk, he filled in all the blanks for me.

During his call with Nicholas last night, Mr. Foster realized that I had a website that features my designs. Nicholas mentioned it when he was telling Gabriel that Claudia wanted to meet me after seeing my work. At the very moment Mr. Foster found the site, Nicholas suggested that I lose my job for what he believes I did to him. Mr. Foster didn't argue the point because he was too busy looking over my designs. He told me he saw my potential immediately. By the time Nicholas abruptly ended their call, Gabriel was already envisioning my work as part of the new Ella Kara collection he's preparing to launch.

"I wasn't technically fired. I accepted a new position within the company." I smile because my new contract includes a mile long list of perks and a healthy raise. As soon as Zoe Beck looks it over and approves it, I'll sign on the dotted line. Until then, I'm shadowing Sasha to get a feel for the process.

"Mr. Foster didn't want you to sell your designs in Claudia's stores, did he? He knows you've got something special. He realizes how much talent you have."

I crack an unexpected smile. "You hit the nail on the head, Den. Today my boss finally saw my potential and I couldn't be happier."

I'm a liar.

I could be happier. I could be celebrating my new job in the arms of Nicholas Wolf tonight. Instead, I'm expecting an attorney to call me at any time to tell me that the man I thought might be my future is taking me to court.

***

I spot her almost instantly inside the boutique that has drawn the attention of virtually every aspiring clothing designer in the country. She's beautiful; tall, regal and wearing a red jumpsuit that would be impossible for most women to pull off. It's not surprising that Claudia Stefano began her career as a model.

Every notable designer in the world wanted her for their shows and print ads. At one point, she was the most in-demand model on the planet. When she stepped away from that to pursue a career in fashion, I knew that one day I'd meet her. Today is that day.

"Can I help you?" A beautiful woman with brown hair and a sprinkle of freckles across her cheeks asks me as she approaches. Her eyes scan my outfit. I left my wool coat back at work since the walk to this boutique is less than half a block.

I would have chosen something else to wear today if I had known that I'd be coming face-to-face with Claudia. I woke up this morning and put on a dress I'd designed more than a year ago. It's pale purple with a narrow black belt. The lines are clean and simple. It's more than enough to impress Sasha, but she's not in the same league as Claudia.

Just as I was organizing my new workstation in the design department, Mr. Foster walked in. The room hushed and as he stalked toward me, the smile on his face gave me a sense of comfort I didn't know I needed until right that second.

I confided in him about Claudia when I went up to his office to brief his temporary assistant earlier today. I repeated the words Nicholas said about Claudia making sure my designs would never see the light of day. It turns out that Gabriel Foster and Claudia Stefano are old friends.

I didn't have to ask him to speak to her on my behalf. He offered to make a call to her immediately.

My new contract with Foster Enterprises prohibits me from showing any of my pieces in her boutiques right at this very moment, but fashion is a fluid industry and now that I'm a designer for Ella Kara, my path will inevitably cross with Claudia's at some point. I have to undo any damage Nicholas has done.

I'm not a thief and the sooner that Claudia knows that, the better.

Saving my relationship with Nicholas may be impossible, but my professional reputation is salvageable and today that's all that matters to me.

Chapter 3

Nicholas

"You've made such a huge fucking mess of your life." Cheyenne chews on the end of a blue plastic pen she pulled out of her purse. "Why did you bring her here, Nick? I thought you confined extracurricular activities to your office."

"She was different. Is different," I correct myself. "Sophia is different than other women I've known."

"You've got that right." She leans both hands on the edge of my desk. "She fucked her way to a million dollar payout and left you in her dust."

I'm the one who left her in my dust. I walked out of Hibiscus two nights ago without a glance back at Sophia. I couldn't look at her. I couldn't stand the thought of a woman I was falling in love with fucking me over that way.

"This is fixable," I say it even though I doubt like hell that it is. My agent, Steve, called me late last night to tell me that the book has been removed from the website that posted it, but excerpts had already gone viral. Erasing its existence from the internet isn't possible. At this point, the manuscript has no value beyond what I'll be awarded if I sue.

Cheyenne's already pointed that out to me. She was at my door at the break of dawn, ranting about how my publisher is primed to pull the plug on my contract. I avoided her calls yesterday and when she turned up in the lobby of my building, I didn't buzz her in. I needed the day to decompress and weigh my options. It turns out that ignoring my publicist was a monumental mistake.

Cheyenne, in her desperation to sweep this under the rug, told the attorney who called her from the publishing house yesterday that I'd given a copy of the book to my girlfriend. That's enough to not only void my contract but to take legal action against me for breach of contract. I'm screwed, and if I'm going down, I'm taking the person responsible for this fucking mess with me.

The problem is I don't know who the hell that is anymore.

Ever since I left Sophia standing in the restaurant, I haven't been able to forget the way she looked. She was shocked. She's either an Oscar-worthy actress or she was telling me the truth when she said she didn't sell the book. The memory of that innocent expression on her face has been gnawing at me ever since. I can't escape the regret I've been feeling about leaping to the conclusion that Sophia was involved in this.

"You're delusional." Cheyenne slams both palms against my desk. "Do you realize how bad this is, Nick? Your career is over."

I know it's bad, but my career isn't going down with this ship. I may lose my contract and all respect I've had in the publishing world, but my words are mine.

I can still write. I can find a new publisher, or I'll publish myself.

"Have you talked to Sophie?"

"Sophia," I enunciate every syllable of her name. "I already told you that I saw her and she denied doing it."

"Did you expect her to confess on the spot?" She shakes her head. "We're meeting our attorney in an hour. He's going to want to know everything you know about this woman. We'll make her pay for what she did to you."

I turn away. I'm not about to jeopardize Sophia's future. She may be the only person, other than me, who had access to that book, but it doesn't add up.

The woman I spent all that time with felt the same connection to me that I felt to her. I'd bet my life on that. She's not capable of doing this to me and in my rush to point the finger of blame at someone, Sophia landed square in my sights.

"Push the meeting back, Cheyenne." I hold up my hand to stop her as she opens her mouth to talk. "Don't fight me on this. I'll meet him later today or tomorrow. I need time to think and I can't do that with an attorney who is itching to file a lawsuit breathing down my neck."

***

An hour later I rake both of my hands through my hair. "This doesn't make any fucking sense to me."

Cheyenne takes a seat on the couch next to Liam. My brother showed up twenty minutes ago with some choice words for me. Emails we shared six months ago popped up on one of the many social media accounts that my fans have created.

Someone tagged Liam and when he read the emails, he left his office and headed straight for me. Who the hell could blame him? They're messages we'd exchanged regarding the woman he was dating at the time. He wanted out of the relationship, but she was emotionally fragile. The fact that she's been texting him non-stop since he got here isn't helping.

"How the hell am I supposed to calm Britney down?" Liam waves his phone at me. "She's a decent girl, Nick. Her dirty laundry is everywhere now."

"No one knows her last name," I point out. I know that for a fact because Wolf never offered it and I never asked. We don't go into details about the women we fuck because they're all temporary hook-ups. When I told him about Sophia a few weeks ago, that was the exception.

"Her friends and family know it's her." His voice is laced with anger. "She's humiliated."

He is too. I see it written all over his expression. Liam keeps to himself. He always has. Exposing him like this is going to damage what we have.

"I'm sorry," I offer even though it's minimal considering the circumstances. "I don't know how it happened, Liam."

"Sophia." Cheyenne reaches to tap Wolf's shoulder through his coat. "Nick's latest is selling his life to the highest bidder as we speak."

I lean back in the chair I'm sitting in. She's dead wrong. There's no way Sophia had access to those emails. When I handed her my laptop, my email program was closed. I use that same email address to send everything to my agent and my contact at the publishing house. I shut it down whenever I'm done using it and I have to enter the password each and every time I log in.

"Cha-ching." Cheyenne gazes down at her phone. "Sophia just added a few more dollars to her nest egg. Every email you've ever shared with Steve is currently being uploaded to one of those trashy gossip websites."

I reach to grab her phone, my eyes dropping to the screen. Email after email written by me to my agent and vice versa floods the screen. Details about my contracts, my future projects and my ongoing complaints about my editor and my contact at the publisher are on full display.

"What the hell?" I mutter under my breath. "Who the fuck is doing this?"

"You know who." Cheyenne yanks her phone from my hands. "I'm not pushing the meeting with the attorney back again, Nick. We're going down there now. Your lover is determined to ruin your life and if you don't put a stop to it, I will."

I curse under my breath. "Fine. I'll meet with him but Sophia's not responsible for these emails. There's no way in hell she'd do this. She didn't do any of this. She's not the one trying to ruin my life."

I absorb my own words as I grab my coat. I'm the one who ruined the best thing that ever happened to me and right now I don't give a shit about anything but talking to Sophia.

Chapter 4

Sophia

I exit the elevator and I'm instantly taken aback by what my old desk looks like. It's covered in file folders, one stained with what looks like coffee. Mr. Foster's temp has called me more than a dozen times already today. It's obvious that she's overwhelmed with the job.

"Nancy," I call out to her as I approach since she's bent over retrieving something from the floor. "Tell me what you need from me."

She jumps in surprise, smashing the back of her head on the corner of the desk.

I cringe as I lunge forward to help, but she's already on her feet, her hand rubbing what must be a tender spot hidden under her red hair. "Sophia, you came."

Of course, I did. Sasha told me that until I sign my contract, I'm a technically still Mr. Foster's assistant, so I'm on call for whatever Nancy needs until the permanent replacement starts next week.

When Nancy called my cell less than five minutes ago to tell me she urgently needed to see me, I tucked my sketchbook into a drawer on my new workstation, and I headed straight for the elevator.

"What can I do for you?" I ask cheerily. She's probably had to deal with Mr. Foster's less than friendly demeanor all day. I know he's frustrated. He said as much in a text message he sent me yesterday telling me he was considering asking Sasha to fire me so he could rehire me.

"It's not me this time." She smiles. "Mr. Foster asked me to find you so he could talk to you."

I glance at the closed door of his office. "He wants to see me?"

"As soon as possible." She pushes on my shoulder. "That means now, Sophia, so get in there."

I laugh nervously. He's already asked me once if I'll be signing the contract for my new position with the design department. I told him I was waiting to get it back from my attorney, which I am. If he brings it up again today, I may need to ask Zoe Beck to put my file at the top of her priority list. I haven't given it as much thought as I should have. I've been replaying what happened with Nicholas in my mind over and over again. I still haven't heard from him or the attorney he threatened me with. I don't know whether that's a good or bad sign.

"Did he say what it was about?"

"Like he'd tell me," she jokes. "All I hear about all day is what a great assistant he had. If I had to wager a guess, it would be that he's going to offer you your old job back. If he does, I think you should take it and start right now."

"Funny." My grin is wide. "I'll go talk to him but you should know that you're stuck here until your replacement shows up next week."

"Damn." She winks. "In that case, it's time for my coffee break."

***

"Has your attorney had a chance to look over the contract yet, Sophia?" Mr. Foster asks as I take a seat. "I'm impressed that you didn't sign it on the spot. It's always prudent to have a professional go over any legal document line-by-line."

I can't argue that point. The wording of the contract went right over my head. It's much more complicated than the standard salary based contract I signed when I started working as his executive assistant. The design contract has strict stipulations regarding how I share my designs and an allowance for travel in the event my pieces are featured in a fashion show.

"I think I should have it back soon, sir. I'll sign it then."

"I'd rather you didn't." He taps his fingers on a large yellow envelope in the center of his desk. "I had a new contract drawn up earlier today. This offer replaces the original one."

Shit. I took too long to sign and now Mr. Foster is pulling back on his offer. That has to be what this is. He may be a great boss, but the man is still a ruthless shark.

"The other contract seemed very fair." I scratch the back of my head. "I'll call my attorney today and see if I can have it signed by tomorrow."

"No." He opens the envelope and draws out a stack of papers. "That offer is no longer on the table. I think you'll find this one benefits you more."

Benefits me more? I hope I get a meal allowance like Sasha does. That woman wasn't the same today when she returned from her two hour long lunch. One of the other designers told me that Sasha dines on the company's dime, which always includes a substantial amount just for several glasses of a good red wine. I could go for a glass or two myself right at this moment.

I scan the top sheet of the papers. "So I should give this one to my attorney and tell her to forget the other one?"

"You should, but first you should ask me why I'm rescinding my original offer."

Of course I should. We're having an important discussion about my future with his company I should keep my mind on that and not on the signed copy of *Burden's Proof* that is sitting on the corner of his desk.

"Why are you rescinding your original offer?" I ask with a small smile.

"Flip that paper over and you'll see why." He turns the entire stack of papers toward me.

I grab the edge of the top sheet and flip it aside. My eyes settle on a logo. It's feminine, elegant and when I read the words, my heart misses a full beat.

"Mr. Foster." I squeeze my eyes shut. "Please tell me this is real."

"Sophia." I feel his hand brush against mine. "This is real. The label of our new collection is now officially *Ella Kara by Sophia Reese.*"

"It's my collection." I open my eyes through a veil of tears. "I'm heading the collection?"

"You own a stake in this." He moves his hand to pick up the papers. "You'll get the monthly stipend we originally offered but you'll also be a shareholder in this line. If you can make it the success I know you can, you'll benefit in every way."

"Why would you do this?" I ask quietly. "Two days ago I was your executive assistant."

He chuckles deeply. "Claudia came to see me after you visited her at the boutique. She's launching a swimwear line and wanted to know if you had any experience in that realm. I told her to speak directly to you, which she will."

"She hasn't yet."

Claudia took my number when I met with her at her boutique. She didn't tell me exactly what Nicholas said to her, but she made it clear that she valued Gabriel's opinion of me more. We briefly talked fashion and my aspirations before she had to speed away to the stockroom to overlook the arrival of a shipment from a designer based in Tennessee.

"I'm grateful for that." He pushes the papers back into the envelope. "I want you at Foster, Sophia. Sasha has told me that she sees more promise in you than in any designer she's worked with in years. I'm giving you this line to show us what you've got. Sasha will work closely with you. You'll run everything by me and when we unveil this, it's going to be your designs the world sees."

Next to launching a line on my own, this is the next best thing. I can get eyes on my creative talent and I don't have to foot the bill. If this isn't the fast track road to success, I don't know what is.

"I thought my career was over two days ago." I wipe a tear from my cheek. "Now my dream is coming true."

"You're going to make me proud." He pushes to stand. "Show this to your attorney and get it signed."

"I'm on it." I take the envelope from him. "Is that all, sir?"

"We're going to be partners in this venture, Sophia. Call me Gabriel from now on."

"Thank you, Gabriel." The words rush out. "I can't tell you how honored I am. I won't let you down."

"I know you won't." He rounds the desk.

I turn to leave but his hand on my elbow stops me.

"One other thing, Sophia."

"Yes?" I pivot on my heel to look at him again. "What is it?"

"Nicholas Wolf was here earlier. He came to talk to me about you."

Hearing his name tenses my stomach. I try to temper my tone. "About me? Why would he do that?"

His hand drops to his side. "He wanted to know if I had indeed fired you."

I don't ask what his response was. Mr. Foster is as honest as they come.

"I didn't give him any details but made it clear that Foster Enterprises stands behind you." He tilts his chin back. "That includes our entire legal team if need be."

I'm stunned by that. I had already asked Zoe what the cost would be if I needed a lawyer to help defend me against the baseless accusations Nicholas threw at me. The price she quoted is more than my parents paid for their house back in Florida.

"Thank you," I mumble, trying to contain my emotion. "I appreciate your support."

"You haven't spoken to him since the night he called me, have you?"

"I doubt I'll ever talk to him again." I sigh. I want to. I want to tell Nicholas that he's made a huge mistake but I can't. It doesn't matter at this point that I'm completely innocent. The mere fact that he believes I'm capable of doing something like that to him is enough for me to wash my hands of the relationship for good. "I want to be with a man who defends my honor; not one who questions it."

"He knows you didn't do it, Sophia. He came here to fight for your job and for you."

Chapter 5

Nicholas

It's after six now. I've been staring at the screen of my phone for almost an hour. I know Sophia's work day ends at five. At least it did when she was an executive assistant. When Gabriel told me yesterday that he moved her over to the design department, I wanted to find her and congratulate her. I didn't. There's no way in hell the woman wants anything to do with me since I tried to destroy her entire life. I jumped to a fucked up conclusion that I should have known couldn't be true.

I want to call her, but I have no idea what the hell I'd say to her.

Sophia's forgiveness is what I want. It's the one and only thing I want right now.

"I'm heading home, Nick." Cheyenne walks back into my living room. She's been on the phone for the past two hours trying to put a positive spin on what's happened. It's a tall task that even she isn't equipped to handle.

By mid-morning today, my lawyer was able to get most of the private emails that were leaked removed from the websites that posted them. By noon he had the name of the person responsible for all of it.

Joe, the tech guy I trusted with my computer, was the asshole who sold my book and then upped the ante by selling my private emails, photographs and whatever the hell else he could from the data he downloaded from my laptop when I asked him to fix a sticky key on the keyboard.

I thought nothing of dropping my computer off with him one afternoon a few weeks ago. When I picked it up, he made an off-handed comment about all the sensitive information on my laptop. I thought he was joking. Apparently, it was a warning.

I made the call to Gabriel Foster once I had confirmation it was Joe. He fired him on the spot and now their tech department is reviewing everything Joe accessed and downloaded. When I last spoke to Gabriel an hour ago, he told me that one of his senior tech guys retraced Joe's digital steps. He didn't access any of the confidential files related to Foster's upcoming designs, but he had a huge interest in the contact information and test shots for the models Foster Enterprises utilizes for their print campaigns.

"Your tech guy is a dick." Cheyenne slides her coat on before she wraps a pink scarf around her neck. "What's going to happen to him?"

"Sebastian said he'll be arrested. It's not his division, but he said it's a clear case." I toss my phone onto the coffee table. "I need to go downtown tomorrow to fill out a statement."

"Do you want me to go with you?"

I shake my head. "You need a day off. I'll catch you later in the week."

"This shows that you can't trust anyone completely." She shoulders her purse. "I thought all along it was Sophia. Your computer guy wasn't even on my radar."

Or mine. He was so far off my radar that I accused Sophia of stealing. If that doesn't make me enough of a prick, I had to up the stakes by calling her boss before I told Claudia to steer clear of her in the future.

"Do you want me to call for a car?" I ignore her comment. The only reason she thought it was Sophia is because I'm the jerk who told her that.

"I'm taking the bus." She takes one step toward the door before she turns to look at me. "Don't beat yourself up over this, Nick. You'll sue Joe and the website that paid him all that money."

"Sure."

"Steve worked his magic and things are good with the publisher. You're going to make it out of this in one piece."

I give her a nod as she turns to leave. I may make it out of this in one piece, but I changed the entire course of my future and Sophia's. I know she's the woman I'm destined to be with and now I'll never get a chance to tell her that.

***

"Go talk to her." Liam pushes on the edge of the empty plate in front of him. "You didn't have to buy me dinner to ask me a question about your girlfriend, Nick."

I weigh how to respond. "She's not my girlfriend, Liam. We never defined our relationship."

He glances over my shoulder. The restaurant he chose is busy for a Wednesday night. It wouldn't be my first choice and it's not just because the food is subpar. People have recognized me all night and even though only two have approached our table, I can feel more than a dozen sets of eyes burning a path through my back at any given second.

I wanted to order in at my place, but Liam was insistent. I met him here and agreed to foot the bill because I still feel guilty about our private emails seeing the light of day.

"You're splitting hairs." He takes a pull from his beer. It's an expensive import that he'd never typically drink. He's making me pay, literally, for not deleting those emails when he asked me to months ago. "You like this girl. If you hadn't fucked it up, she'd be your girlfriend. She was that before all this went down."

She was. I viewed her that way and I believe Sophia considered herself my girlfriend. The title doesn't matter. What does matter is the way I feel about her. "Tell me how to fix this."

"I specialize in grief counseling." He brushes his hair from the side of his face. "I'm not an expert on situations where one lover accuses another of stealing their unpublished manuscript. I read it, by the way. It's brilliant as usual."

I take the compliment with a smile. It would have done well if I had been given the opportunity to release it. "Thanks, Wolf. I appreciate that you took the time to read a pirated copy of my book."

He laughs. The sound is rich and warm. "You lost a few million in that, didn't you?"

That's a low estimate. The advance alone was near eight figures. "Around that. I'll recoup some one day if this thing goes to court or it settles before it comes to that."

"You're lucky you've got a big bank account to fall back on."

I swallow a mouthful of the wine I ordered with my dinner. "Whatever I recover I'll donate. The book is out there now. I might as well turn this into something positive."

"You're a good man, Nick."

"Tell me how to convince Sophia I am."

He finishes the last swallow of his beer. "Start with an apology."

Chapter 6

Sophia

I stare at the soft blanket in Cadence's hands. It's the first gift I've given her for Firi. She hasn't said one word since I handed it to her. I'm beginning to wonder if I should have gone to the store she's registered at and chosen something that she actually needs instead of this.

"You don't like it," I say. It's not a question. I don't want to give her an out. I'd rather just state the obvious so we can move on.

She shakes her head slightly.

I tug at the corner of the blanket. "I'll get you something else, Den. I'm sorry. I just thought you'd like this. Obviously, I suck at making things for a baby."

"Don't." Her voice cracks. "Don't take it back."

My best friend rarely wears her heart on her sleeve, but right now she is. I recognize the quake in her tone.

"I love it," she continues. "I can't believe you'd do this for me."

I suck in a sharp breath. I don't want to cry. If I do, I already know that my tears of joy for Cadence will morph into something else quickly. I've been on the precipice of an emotional meltdown for days and I'm not about to let it happen right now. "I wanted to make something special for the baby."

"You didn't throw out my old baby clothes." Her hand runs over one of the patterned rectangles that make up the blanket's border. "This is that pink dress I told you I wore when I was three-years-old."

It is. When we were still living together, Cadence's mom had come for a visit along with a trunk full of keepsakes from when Den was a kid. Inside were old report cards, a catcher's mitt and a bag filled with clothing that Cadence wore when she was an infant and toddler.

Many of the pieces were too worn to save for another generation, so Cadence made the decision to toss them in the trash. I told her I'd take the bag down to the dumpster, but I kept it. I hid it in the back of my closet because to me they were treasures that I knew I'd eventually make use of. I had no idea back then that many of the pieces I salvaged from her old sleepers, dresses, and T-shirts would become a blanket for her first child.

"I know there's a lot of pink in it." I laugh. "But I added some odds and ends I had to make it at least a little more masculine."

"It's everything, Soph." She reaches for my hand. "You don't know how perfect this is. I can't wait to show my mom."

She won't have to wait long. I spoke to her mom just this morning about her surprise visit next week. She hasn't seen Cadence since she found out she was pregnant and now that the nursery is almost complete, it's the perfect time for Firi's grandma to come to town.

"I'm glad you like the blanket." I glance down at my watch. "I made a reservation for us at seven. You're sure you're not too tired for our dinner?"

She gingerly lays the blanket across the back of her couch. "My best friend is the lead designer on what is going to be the fashion line everyone is talking about this fall. That calls for a celebration. I'm not bailing on you, Sophia."

"You're just excited to see Tyler." I slip into my coat.

"I didn't choose Nova for our celebration dinner because of my fiancé." She picks up her coat from where she slung it over a chair. "I chose it because the food is the best in the city."

She's right about that. "I'm going to have the striped sea bass."

"You should look at the new menu before you decide."

"I don't need to." I slip my arm around her waist. "It's my favorite meal and I'm going to enjoy it with my favorite person in the world."

She wraps her arms around me. "I love you, Soph. I've never been more proud of anyone. By this time next year, everyone is going to know exactly who Sophia Reese is."

***

"Sophia?"

His voice sends a shiver down my spine. I haven't heard it since that night at Hibiscus. I've missed its textured nuances. I've missed him.

I turn on my heel. He's less than a foot behind me. "Nicholas."

"I saw you leaving Nova with Cadence." His gaze jerks from my face to my hands. "I had dinner at a place down the block from there."

I don't ask who he had dinner with because it doesn't matter anymore. Nothing matters except the fact that he called me a thief.

"I don't think we should be talking to each other." I fish in my purse for my phone. "I have a lawyer. I can give you her number. I think you should be talking to her."

"Why would I need to talk to your lawyer?"

I scan the contact list of my phone, searching for Zoe's number. "I have the right to remain silent."

He huffs out a laugh. "I'm not arresting you."

"I know. You're suing me. My lawyer would tell me not to talk to you," I shoot back, annoyed that he's finding humor in this.

"Your lawyer doesn't know what I want to say to you," he says smoothly.

I roll my eyes. "It doesn't matter what you want to say; you need to say it to my lawyer. That's not hard to understand, Nicholas. Her name is Zoe Beck. Her number is…"

"I don't want her number." He steps even closer. He's so close that I can smell the scent of his skin. "I want to tell you that I'm sorry. I need to tell you I regret everything I said to you that night and I want you to understand that I'll do whatever it takes to make this up to you."

Chapter 7

Nicholas

She bites her red stained bottom lip as she stares at me.

"I'm sorry, Sophia," I continue since she's not saying a word. "I was a royal asshole to you that night. I did shit I'm not proud of. I look back now and I can't believe I accused you of that."

"I can't believe it either." She sighs. "I'm not capable of stealing anything from anyone."

"I realize that." I want to reach out and touch her, but I stop myself. It's not just because we're in the middle of a crowded sidewalk. It's because her body language is screaming at me to fuck right off. "I wasn't thinking clearly."

"I appreciate the apology." She takes a step closer to the curb. "I'm going to find a cab and head home now."

She's as cold as ice. Her expression hasn't faltered, her voice hasn't given away anything about what she's feeling inside.

"Can we talk more about what happened?" I move toward the curb too. "I need you to understand where my head was at."

She glances over my shoulder at the oncoming traffic. "There's nothing to talk about."

"There's a lot to talk about," I argue. "I fucked this up. I want a chance to make it better."

A smile tugs at the corner of her lips. "I don't want to discuss anything with you."

The grin on her face isn't because I followed her down the street so I could grovel. It's because she thinks I'm fucking pathetic to assume she wants another chance to be with me. She's right. I stomped all over her heart and called her boss to get her fired. I admit I'm not the definition of a good boyfriend.

"I care about you," I say that because I've gotten nothing else waiting on the tip of my tongue.

That prompts a raise of both of her brows. "Don't go there."

"Go where?"

She crosses her arms over her chest. "Don't think you can tell me you care about me after what you did. It's obvious you don't, so I'm prepared to let our lawyers figure this out between themselves."

"I don't need a lawyer to tell you that I'm crazy about you."

"Why are you doing this?" She glances at a couple arm-in-arm as they stroll past us. "You think I stole your book. You're going to sue me. We can't exactly sleep together while that's going on, can we?"

I swallow. A vivid vision of the last time we fucked envelops me. I instantly recall the smell of her skin, the taste of her lips and the sounds she made when she came around my cock. I want that again but more than that, I want her to look at me the way she had before I saw her at Hibiscus.

"Give me thirty minutes, Sophia."

"I'm going home, Nicholas." She waves her hand in the air at an approaching yellow cab.

"Can it be another night?" I step to the curb as the taxi slows. "Give me thirty minutes one night this week."

"Is this about the lawsuit?" She steps onto the street.

"I'm not suing you." I follow her lead and reach for the handle of the passenger side door of the cab. "I'm sorry I threatened you with that. It was wrong."

"You're not suing me?" Her voice softens. "I should thank you for that but I won't because it was baseless and if you had sued me, I would have countersued you."

I know she would have and there's no way in hell she wouldn't have won. I should be the one thanking her for not dragging my ass to court.

"Give me thirty minutes to plead my case. I promise that's all I want."

I want more. I want much more but I'll take thirty minutes of her time if that's all I can get right now.

She smiles at the cab driver before she slips into the back seat. "I'll text you if I find the time to meet."

"When you find the time," I correct her. "You'll text me when you find the time."

"It may not be for days." She reaches for the handle of the door even though I'm still leaning against it. "I'm busy so it could be weeks."

"I'll wait forever," I say before I shut the door and watch the car speed away with Sophia inside.

***

"You can't write an email worth shit, Nick," Crew says as he picks up the tumbler of bourbon I poured him.

"What the hell does that mean?" I furrow my brow. "I take it you read my emails that were posted online?"

"They were boring as hell." He takes a sip of the drink. "I had to bail after three of them. Thank Christ you can write a book. If you had to rely on your email writing skills to bring home the bacon, you'd be camped out on my couch."

That wouldn't be a bad thing. I've been to Crew's apartment. I thought my place was the definition of luxury. Compared to Crew's, I'm living modestly. "They were never meant for public consumption."

"You're telling me." He leans forward to place the glass on the coffee table. "In all seriousness, I want to introduce you to a guy I know. I think he could help you out."

"With what?" I ask suspiciously. I trust Crew but in my personal experience when anyone tells you they know a guy, it's always because they think you need a hand. The only thing I need help with is getting Sophia to listen to me.

"You need a better negotiator than your agent." He exhales harshly. "From what I read in those emails, that guy isn't going to bat for you. He's settling and you're worth more. If you want someone who can get you what you deserve, I'll set up a meeting between you two."

I've been considering ending my agreement with Steve for some time so I'm open to the idea. "Is he an agent?"

"He does a little of everything." He barks out a laugh. "Take the meeting and get a feel for him. If you two click, you can give me a ten percent finder's fee on the first contract he negotiates for you."

I cock a brow. "I'll buy you a bottle of scotch and we'll call it even."

"That's a deal." His fingers drum against his knee. "You're a better negotiator than your agent. Maybe you should skip the meeting and work out your own deals."

"Speaking of meetings," I segue into the real reason I invited him over. "I asked Sophia if she'd meet me for thirty minutes last week and I haven't heard a word from her since."

"Do you blame her?" He glances at his watch. "I'm not through foreplay in thirty. You need to learn to pace yourself."

I shake my head. "You're a fucking jerk."

"No." He leans forward, resting his elbows on his thighs. "You're the fucking jerk. I know what you said to her. You're damn lucky I'm your friend too, Nick. If I weren't, I'd take you to task for what you did."

I assumed Sophia had told him but when I called him earlier to ask him to stop by on his way home from work, he seemed fine. Apparently, he's not. I get it. They're friends and he's right to defend her.

"I was wrong," I admit easily. "I fucked up what I had with her. I want it back."

"It's not that simple." His gaze narrows. "Sophia's special. She's also smart. If she thinks a situation is bad for her, she'll avoid it at all costs."

I still. "You think I'm bad for her?"

He doesn't back down. Instead, he leans forward, his finger pointing directly at me. "I think your ego got in the way of what could have been a great thing for you both. You need to check it at that door if you want another chance, but I'm warning you. Don't fuck her around again. If she lets you back in, that'll be your last chance. She won't put up with your bullshit again."

I know he's right. "You think I have another chance?"

"You broke her in two, Nick, and do you know what the first words out of her mouth were the day after you tried to ruin her fucking life?"

"What?"

"She called me to ask if you were okay. She was worried about you. So, yeah, I think you've got a shot at another chance. Make it count. Sophia's one in a million."

Chapter 8

Sophia

"The only thing I hate more than this is…" I tilt my head as I watch him intently. "I can't think of anything. I hate this more than anything else on the face of this earth."

He straightens, the black T-shirt he's wearing pulls taut over his muscular chest. My eyes scan his arms and the colorful tattoos that cover his skin. I checked out his website when I found out that I was going to meet him today. Noah Foster may be one of the most sought after photographers in the country, but he's also one of the most intimidating. It's not just that he's tall with broad shoulders. The jagged scar that covers his face tells a story that he's not willing to. He was hurt at some point, but that's not evident in the tone of his voice or the gentle way he's been guiding me.

"You'll survive, Sophia." He tosses me a smile from where he's standing three feet in front of me. "Try and loosen up. Think of something that makes you happy."

The only thing I've been able to think about since I walked into his studio is Nicholas. It's not just because I can't get my mind off the man. Nicholas owns a Noah Foster original photograph. I saw it hanging in the foyer of his apartment the first time I was there. It's a tasteful shot of a woman. Her face isn't visible, but the curves and contours of her nude body are. It's breathtaking.

"I used to follow your work," I say it before I realize that it's a backhanded compliment. "What I meant to say is that I always thought the photographs you took a few years ago were breathtaking."

The corner of his mouth twitches. "The photographs I take now are breathtaking too. It's just in a much different way."

I know he's right. All of the galleries on his website feature work he's completed recently. In addition to the gorgeous selection of portraits of notable New York residents, he has an entire online portfolio devoted to people in the city who don't have a home of their own. Those pictures, in particular, are filled with turbulent emotions. The joy mixed with sorrow in the faces of his subjects is mesmerizing.

"Gabriel told me you used to work for him." He fills the silence in this studio with his words. "What kind of a boss is my cousin?"

"He's the best," I say quietly. "I learned a lot from him and now he's given me the chance of a lifetime."

"When he called to ask me to handle your portrait, I was honored." He points the camera in his hands at me before he looks through the viewfinder. "He doesn't usually handle stuff like that himself." He's right. It's always been my job to book photo shoots for the designers that come on board. I've spoken to Noah's assistant more than once when I've reached out looking for an opening in his schedule so he could handle a portrait session. I never thought I'd be the one in front of his camera.

"He's always spoken very highly of you, Noah."

"Gabriel's one of the good ones." He snaps a picture. "This is a test shot so don't flip the fuck out."

I laugh aloud. I haven't tried to hide my nervous agitation. I don't like having my picture taken. I never have. I was the kid in grade school who would perfectly time a stomach ache so she could stay home in bed on photo day. I can't avoid this. The portrait Noah takes today is going to be included in all the promo material Foster Enterprises distributes during the pre-launch period for the Ella Kara collection.

"I'm not like the other people you photograph," I hesitate briefly. "I saw all the famous faces on your website."

"Do you know any of them?" He takes a series of pictures while I lean forward on the stool he sat me on when I arrived. He didn't let me fix my hair or my makeup. His assistant brushed a piece of lint from the front of the red dress I'm wearing before she took a seat at a small desk, her eyes trained to a laptop that instantly displays every picture he's taking.

"Nicholas Wolf," I say evenly. "I've met him."

"You've more than met him." He snaps another picture. I glance at his assistant's laptop screen to see if my mouth is hanging open the way I expect it to be. It's not.

"What's that supposed to mean?" My eyes narrow. I know for a fact that there was no inflection in my tone when I said the name of the man who singlehandedly tried to fuck up my entire life. Noah can't know anything unless Gabriel said something which is highly unlikely since Mr. Foster doesn't discuss personal things very often. He hasn't mentioned Nicholas at all to me recently other than when he told me he fired Joe because he was the one who stole the book.

"Gabriel told me about you and Nick." Noah moves closer, the faint sound of the shutter of his camera fills the air as he rapidly takes one picture after another of my face. "He said you two were dating until recently. He's obsessed with Nick's books. When he found out I had photographed Nick last year for his book cover, Gabriel was pissed that I didn't ask for an autographed copy of *Burden's Proof*."

"He has one now." I sweep my hair from my forehead. "I feel like my hair is a mess. I think my headshot should be polished."

He reaches forward to move my hair back to where it was. "Your headshot should be reflective of who you are, Sophia. I'd say your hair is perfect."

I take it as a compliment because I just want this photo shoot to be over.

"Nick's a good guy." He takes half a step back. "When I first met him he asked about my wife. He wanted to know how I found someone in this city who didn't give a shit that I was the Noah Foster."

"He did?" I'm mildly surprised by that. I know that Nicholas had a reputation before we met. I also know that since we stopped seeing each other, it's highly likely that there are a few more of his books floating around Manhattan with lunch invitations written on the inside of the front cover. He seems like the type who would get over a woman in ten seconds flat.

"He did," he confirms. "You don't give a shit that he's Nicholas Wolf, do you?"

"I don't." I shake my head slowly.

"He's the one who fucked up what you two had going on. I know I'm right."

I smile and nod slowly. "You're right."

"He's an idiot." He lifts the camera up again to eye level. "You remind me a lot of my wife. You're genuine. You have an honest soul."

"That's quite the compliment." I don't know a lot about his wife, Alexa, other than what Gabriel has mentioned in passing. I know she's a teacher and just as devoted to her kids as she is to her husband.

"One day he'll realize that you're the one who got away. I fucked things up with Alexa once. By God's grace, I got her back and I can tell you that I'd eat glass for that woman. Nick will come around too."

I want to tell him that he's making assumptions he shouldn't, but I stop myself. I'm here for one reason and one reason only. I need a new portrait. I don't need to talk about Nicholas. He's my past and the portrait, and what it represents, is my future.

Chapter 9

Nicholas

Two weeks. It's been two fucking weeks since I saw Sophia on the street outside Nova. I've been sending her text messages at least once a day since. Her one or two-word responses may vary slightly from day-to-day but they're always followed by the goddamn smiley face emoji which I've come to realize is her subtle way of flipping me off.

Her excuse is always that she's too busy or she already has plans.

She's stubborn, but so am I.

I've filled my time with plotting and outlining my next release. The book that was leaked online will still be sold but at a reduced price with all the proceeds going to a scholarship fund for students who want to pursue a degree in creative writing. It's not an ideal situation, but at least the time I devoted to writing the book won't be a total waste.

"Nicholas?"

I hear Gabriel's voice as he exits his office. I've been sitting in the reception area with his new assistant waiting for him to end a conference call. She's the one who called me late yesterday afternoon to tell me that Gabriel wanted to see me. The only thing we have in common beyond my books is Sophia, so I told his assistant I'd be at his office bright and early to meet with him.

"Gabe." I stand and extend my hand. "It's good to see you."

It is good to see him. It would be better to see Sophia. It's been pure torture being in this building knowing that she's here as well.

"Do you want a coffee? We can get you a bottle of water if you'd prefer." He tosses his assistant a look that instantly draws her to her feet.

"What do you take in your coffee, Mr. Wolf?" She eyes me eagerly. She spoke briefly about *Burden's Proof* when I first arrived. I used an incoming text message from Liam as an out; keeping my gaze focused on my phone until her voice finally trailed off and I heard the urgent rap of her fingers against her keyboard.

"Cream, no sugar." I don't glance at her. "What do you need, Gabe?"

"Follow me." He leads the way to his office, leaving the door open. "Have a seat."

I do. I'm tired as shit. My head didn't hit my pillow until just past four this morning. I was up at eight so I could make it here by nine sharp.

He rounds his desk and takes the seat behind it. He looks good there. He's comfortable in this environment. It's a life I never wanted. I need the freedom of setting my own hours and guiding my career, not worrying about the livelihoods of hundreds of other people.

"Here's your coffee, Nick." The new assistant, whose name I didn't bother to get, places a white ceramic mug filled with steaming coffee in my hands. "If you need anything else, you know exactly where to find me."

Gabriel quirks his brow as she turns to leave. "Shut the door behind you, Ms. Allen."

"How's she working out?" I take a sip of the coffee. It's bitter.

"I want Sophia back."

His words resonate with me. I feel the same way for glaringly different reasons. "Ms. Allen isn't cutting it?"

"I'm convinced she lied on her resume." He exhales. "I'll give her another month. If things don't improve, she'll be replaced."

The words are as clear as the expression on his face. I knew Sophia was good at her job, but this conversation reinforces just how good. Her understanding of fashion and her ability to anticipate what her boss wanted at any given second made her completely irreplaceable in his eyes. He'll struggle to find someone as competent as her because the bar has been set so high.

"How's Sophia doing in her new position?"

Sitting back in his chair, he studies my face. "I take it things between you two are still at a stalemate?"

That's a polite way of saying I'm still being shut out of her life. "We haven't had a chance to connect in a few weeks."

He knows why. I forced him into the middle of my mission to destroy Sophia's life. Since that night, I've replayed the conversation we had over and over in my mind. He was hesitant to believe me. I heard it in his voice and it was there in the silence before I ended the call. I should be grateful I didn't convince him to fire her.

"That's about to change."

"How so?" I take another swallow of the coffee before I push the mug aside.

"Did she fuck up the coffee?" He sighs. "She drinks at least a dozen cups a day so I assumed she'd be an expert at that, at least."

My eyes scan the length of his desk. There's not a coffee cup in sight. "It's not the worst I've ever had."

I didn't drag my ass out of bed to discuss his assistant's coffee brewing skills, so I press on. "You mentioned Sophia."

I leave it open-ended so he can take the lead. I want to talk to Sophia and if Gabe is my in, I'm not about to let that opportunity slip past me.

"I'm planning a small gathering to celebrate the creation of the Ella Kara line. It's mostly industry people attending but I wanted you to know that your name is already on the guest list."

"When and where?"

"Friday night. I've booked a new restaurant for the night. It's called Hibiscus. Do you know it?"

If that's not irony in its finest form, I don't know what the fuck is. "I'll be there."

"I'll have Ms. Allen email you the details."

"Good." I push to stand. "I didn't need to come down for this. I know you're a busy man. You're welcome to call me whenever you want."

His face lights up. I know he'll respect the boundaries of common decency. I don't expect a deluge of calls from the CEO of a worldwide conglomerate. "Sit, Nick. You're about to understand why I called you down here for this."

I move to sit just as there's a soft knock at the door of his office.

"Come in," he calls loudly across the room.

I turn toward the door and as it opens, my heart rate rises. It's her. Sophia, dressed in a stylish black dress with her hair piled loosely on top of her head, stops in place as her eyes meet mine.

Chapter 10

Sophia

Son of a bitch.

I say that to myself. Mr. Foster tricked me. He goddamn tricked me into coming to his office at nine fifteen because he knew damn well Nicholas Wolf would be here.

Shit. He looks better than I remember. He must have rolled out of bed and came straight here. His hair, the growth of beard on his chin and that sleepy, all-too-sexy look in his eyes are all dead giveaways.

I shake the thought of Nicholas in his bed out of my mind.

"You asked to see me, sir?" I shift my gaze from the man I once thought I loved to the man I temporarily loathe. Mr. Foster isn't a matchmaker and he shouldn't be playing one on a random Monday morning.

"I did, Sophia. I wanted to go over the two designs you submitted to Sasha last week."

I already know how much Sasha loves those designs. She told me as much this morning when I got in. Since I signed my new employment contract, it's been full steam ahead on the launch of the Ella Kara line. I've worked tirelessly on not only creating designs but on sewing samples so that Sasha and Mr. Foster have a clear understanding of my vision.

"I came come back later if you're busy." My voice shakes. It's not surprising. I've been avoiding Nicholas for the past two weeks. Every single time he sends me a text message, I fire one back to him telling him that I'm too busy to meet. It's not a complete lie. Ella Kara is my life at the moment and since the launch is only a couple of months away, I need to have six outfits in place, approved and ready for the manufacturer before we unveil the collection to the press.

"Nicholas was just leaving."

I turn to look at him. His brows lift in surprise. Apparently, he wasn't aware that his meeting with Gabriel is over.

I step aside to allow Nicholas room to pass me after he stands. "It's always a pleasure to see you, Gabe."

I bite back a laugh at the expression on Mr. Foster's face. He relishes whatever this is that is going on between him and his favorite author. "I'll see you soon."

"You can count on that." Nicholas moves toward me. "It's good to see you, Sophia."

It's good to see him too and painful. My stomach bunches as he brushes past me and exits the office without another word to me.

***

"You look so fucking hot right now." Dexie eyes me as I enter the living room of my apartment. "Can you believe we are going to a party to celebrate your fashion line?"

I can't. I've tried wrapping my brain around it since Mr. Foster told me about it during our meeting on Monday morning. I was still reeling from seeing Nicholas when I found out that I'd be attending a get together of some of the most influential professionals in the fashion industry. I've literally had to pinch myself more than once to make sure this isn't a dream.

I glance down at the simple red dress I chose to wear. It's a new design for me. It's fitted with a cut out back. It's too daring to wear to work, but it's perfect for tonight. Dexie helped me pull my hair into a tight, high ponytail. The entire look is sleek and sexy. It screams successful fashion designer.

"Is Cadence meeting us there?" The excitement in Dexie's voice is palpable. I invited her as my plus one as soon as I got back to my workstation on Monday. I also told her that I'd need a clutch to carry with me tonight. This may be a party to celebrate the impending launch of my collection, but I want eyes on Dexie's designs too.

"She'll be there. Tyler's coming too."

I didn't have to ask Mr. Foster if there was room for them. Cadence received a formal email invitation from Mr. Foster's new assistant on Monday. My parents did too but the cost of coming here from Florida on such short notice made the trip impossible for them. I promised my mom I'd take loads of pictures and send them to her tomorrow.

"What about Nicholas?" Dexie wiggles her perfectly shaped brows. She looks gorgeous tonight. Her small frame tucked into a sleek black dress I designed just for her. Her pink hued hair is in loose waves that cascade down her shoulders and onto her back.

"What about him?" I bite back as I fasten my mom's silver watch to my wrist.   "He's a writer. He doesn't know the first thing about fashion."

"He's a part of your life," she points out.

"Was a part of my life," I correct her quickly. "This night is all about me and my accomplishments. My current success has nothing to do with him."

That's not entirely true. If Nicholas hadn't freaked the fuck out and called Mr. Foster because he thought I stole his book, I wouldn't be the head of the Ella Kara collection. It's a bare truth that I think about every single day. His rantings lead Mr. Foster to my website and the rest is history.

"We're going to be late if we don't head out now." She taps the face of my watch. "The last time you were at Hibiscus is going to be a distant memory after tonight."

I confided in Dexie about my reservations about stepping foot in that restaurant again. It's filled with the bad taste of the angry words that Nicholas was throwing at me. She's right though. Tonight will change everything for me. This is my new slate and I'm ready to make the most of it.

Chapter 11

Sophia

Ever since I've understood the concept of high fashion, I've followed the careers of the trailblazers in the industry. I'd read every magazine I could get my hands on and study the designs that the world was talking about. Then I'd hide away in my bedroom in my parents' home in Florida and use those pieces as my inspiration.

I never copied what anyone else was doing. Even back then, I knew that creativity is born from within and every person who presses the tip of a pencil to a sketchpad needs to find themselves in their designs.

I'd sketch page after page of dresses, skirts, and tops and then at the end of each month, I'd trash most. I'd always choose one as my favorite and when I'd gather enough money from babysitting the neighbor's kids, I'd go to the fabric store and buy whatever was discounted.

Then I'd work after school and on weekends on creating my design. I'd take buttons from the jar of odds-and-ends my mother and I would find on the ground whenever we were out. I'd rip zippers out of my brother's old hand-me-downs to use to fasten the dresses I'd sew.

When I'd wear those items to school, I'd draw the attention of my classmates. Sometimes their glances were accompanied with compliments but more often than not it was insults and giggles that were leveled at me.

I didn't change. I'd design, sew and wear my own clothing because I knew deep in my soul that one day I'd be in New York City launching my own collection. What I couldn't have imagined is that I'd be in a room with so many people I idolize.

"This is all for you, Soph." Cadence wraps her arm around my shoulder. "I can't stop crying."

She hasn't stopped since I got here. I saw her across the restaurant when I first arrived. She towers over most when she wears heels and it's easy for her and Tyler to stand out in a crowd. They're a beautiful couple, especially tonight. He's dressed in a gray suit and she's wearing a maternity dress that I know was designed by Evlin Dawn.

She apologized profusely in a text message earlier but I told her that I understand. If she could, Cadence would be proudly wearing one of the dresses I made for her to this event, but she can't. The designer label that's sewn into her blue dress doesn't change how much I love her or how grateful I am that she's here on the most important night of my life.

"It's overwhelming." I lean into her. "Sometimes I feel like I'm living a dream."

I feel her breath hitch, so I look up at her face. "Did the baby kick?"

She shakes her head slowly, her eyes glued to the entrance of the restaurant.

I turn to look but I don't see anything but a steady stream of unfamiliar people walking through the door. "Do you see someone you know?"

She nods, her mouth closed tightly.

"It's not your ex, is it?" I inch up to my tiptoes, using her arm as leverage. "You had that same look on your face when we saw him at the movies last month."

"It's not him." She tugs me closer. "It's your ex, Soph. Nicholas Wolf is here."

***

"This party is invitation only, Nicholas."

He slides his index finger over the screen of his phone and turns it toward me. I scan the view and instantly realize it's the same email Cadence and my parents received. He's on the guest list which means Mr. Foster is behind this.

"I'll leave if you'd prefer," he offers. "For the record, I'd like to stay."

"For the record, I'm still mad at you," I bite back through a smile. People are looking in our direction and I know it's not because I'm the head of Ella Kara's design team. It's because Nicholas Wolf, author extraordinaire, just walked into the restaurant.

"I'd like to discuss that." His hand rises in the air as he waves at someone.

He looks way too good in a suit. I try not to focus on that and let my ever present anger take the reins. "Not here."

"I agree." He swallows hard. "What about after this? There's a quiet bar near here that we can go to."

I should say no. There's no reason why we need to talk. He destroyed me emotionally the last time we were in this restaurant together. "I don't think that's a good idea, Nicholas. What we had is over. We can't go back."

He steps closer to allow a server, carrying a tray of champagne flutes, to pass behind him. "I don't want it to be over. I fucked up. I own that but I can make this right again."

I don't know how. It's not that I can't forgive him for what he said. Words are words and sometimes the pain they cause is deep but I've always been able to move past anything said to me in anger by someone I care for.

What I can't get over is the fact that he believed that I was responsible for the leak of his book.

"I don't think that's possible," I whisper. "You don't even know me."

"I know me," he counters. "I know that I felt exposed and vulnerable. I know I lashed out at you without considering who you are. I regretted what I said to you immediately, Sophia. I knew that I'd made a mistake before I left this place."

I glance around the room. "I don't think we can come back from this."

"Do you want to?"

"Do I want to?" I parrot back. "What does that mean?"

His hand brushes my forearm. "Do you want to try and rebuild this? Are you open to giving me another chance?"

"I can't answer that," I say honestly. "I thought what we had was special. I felt a lot of things when we were together. Now, I feel let down and bitter."

"Sophia." I hear a deep voice call my name from behind me. "Come here. I want you to meet someone."

"Gabriel needs me." I don't look at Nicholas. "I have to go."

"I'll be waiting by the door at midnight. I've told you before I just want thirty minutes, Sophia. Give me that."

I glance back over my shoulder to where Gabriel is standing next to a woman I don't immediately recognize. When I turn back, Nicholas is staring down at me. "I'll have one drink with you, Nicholas. You can say your peace and then this is over."

A smile ghosts his perfect lips. "I'll count every second until midnight."

I will too. In three hours, I'll be sitting face-to-face with the man who broke my heart.

Chapter 12

Nicholas

It's do-or-die for me at this moment. I have one chance to convince Sophia that I'm the man for her. I've watched her all night. She confidently moved through the crowd, talking to countless people. Her gaze never wandered from the face of the individual she was engaged in a conversation with. She took her time, smiled, laughed and then at the end of the night, gave an eloquent, off-the-cuff speech about what fashion has meant to her life.

If there was any doubt that I was in love with her before tonight, it's been erased.

This is the woman I want in my life. She's everything I need and more.

Now, all I have to do is get her to understand that I'm not the man who stood in front of her in one of the private rooms of this restaurant a few weeks ago. I'm not the guy who spat out hate-fueled words.

"Your thirty minutes starts now, Nicholas." She glances down at her watch.

"It'll start after we order a drink." I push open the door of the restaurant to allow her to step through and onto the sidewalk. Most of the partygoers have already left, but there are still a few people hanging back to enjoy the free drinks and food supplied by Foster Enterprises.

"I set the rules." She tosses me a look over her shoulder. "I say your time starts now."

I won't argue. I saw the hesitation on her face when I caught her eye at five minutes to midnight. I thought she might bail although if she had, I would have argued my case.

"Now it is." I rest my hand on the small of her back to guide her down the street. "We're going to that bar over there. A friend of mine owns it."

That's not meant to impress her. It's not a warning either. The owner is a woman, twice my age who is close friends with my mother. I don't want Sophia to question the embrace I'll receive when I walk through the door.

It happens as if on cue. Shirley Bartlett rushes toward me the moment Sophia and I step through the nondescript glass door of the small establishment. It's been a neighborhood staple for years. It's also where I took my first swallow of a cheap whiskey that burned my throat. I was fifteen at the time and the memory of that day, sitting next to my father at the bar, is as vivid now as it was then.

"Nicky." She yanks me toward her. "Look at you. You're a big deal now."

Sophia eyes me up before her gaze moves to Shirley. The long dark braid down her back is a signature look for her. That and the dark rimmed glasses she's always wearing.

"Shirley Bartlett, I want you to meet Sophia Reese."

Sophia smiles shyly. "It's nice to meet you, Ms. Bartlett."

"Shirley. You'll call me Shirley like the rest of the world does."

Sophia nods before her gaze drops to her watch.

My time with her is rapidly running out, so I scan the space for an open table. "We'll take that back table, Shirl. I'll have my regular and Sophia will have a glass of red wine."

"White wine," Sophia corrects me. "Tonight I'm drinking white wine."

I smile. "White wine it is. A glass from your best bottle, Shirley."

"House white is fine." Sophia smirks.

"This is her, isn't it?" Shirley turns to face me directly. "This is the girl your mama told me about. This is the fashion designer."

Sophia shuffles on her feet.

"Yes," I answer clearly. "This is her. Sophia is the woman my mom told you about. She's the most incredible woman I've ever known."

***

"What I said to Shirley is true. You are the most incredible woman I've ever known."

She traces her index finger around the rim of her wine glass. "I guess I should thank you for the compliment."

She hasn't said a word to me since we sat down. We waited in silence for Shirley to bring our drinks and then as she went on about a conversation she had earlier today with my mom, I listened fully aware that every second was eating into my time with Sophia. I finally asked Shirley to give us a minute and she did without question.

"I'm sorry, Sophia."

Her gaze trails over my face. I see the sadness in her eyes. It's been there since that night at Hibiscus when I accused her of the unimaginable. "I know that you are."

My heart buoys with her words even though I know she's the forgiving type. She's more compassionate than most people. I saw that tonight when she gave a piece of herself to everyone at her party. "I should have taken some time to decompress after I found out the book was made public. I was angry and when I lashed out, that was completely wrong. There's no excuse for the way I treated you."

She nods. "I get that you were upset about your book showing up online, Nicholas. What I don't get is how you jumped to the conclusion that I was responsible for that."

It's a fair question. I know she's not referring to the fact that at the time I believed that the only two people who had access to that file were the two of us. She wants to know how I thought she was capable of something so underhanded. "I wasn't thinking straight. I was panicked. I didn't take a minute to think about the woman I had spent all that time with."

"You only considered the cold, hard facts?"

"It's all I could see in front of me at the time," I say truthfully before I take a swallow of whiskey to fuel my next words. "I was enraged. It took months to write that book and in an instant, I lost all that effort."

"And money," she adds. "I know you must have lost a lot."

"Money is money." I sigh. "Whatever I do get from the book is going directly to charity."

She rubs the back of her neck, the motion shifting the front of her dress, exposing a sliver of the side of her right breast. "That's generous of you."

"It feels right to me. It's a shitty situation but if something positive comes of it, I'll be happy."

"You're a good person."

I can't tell if that's surprise that laces her voice or not, so I take her words at face value. "I am a good person. I fucked up. I've regretted it since that night."

"It showed that you don't trust me." She takes a sip of wine; her lips leave a faint imprint of red lipstick on the glass. My cock stirs at the sight. I want that lipstick on me. On my lips, my jaw, my chest, and rimmed around my dick.

"I trust you, Sophia."

"No." She shakes her head. "I'm sorry but I don't believe you."

"I trust you more than anyone I've ever known."

She chuckles softly. "Words are just words, Nicholas. Your actions that night say otherwise."

"Let me prove it to you."

"How would you do that?" The tip of her index finger traces the outline of her earlobe. "You can't prove to me that you trust me."

"I'll bare my soul to you." I pat the center of my chest. "I know you have questions about me, about my life. Ask and I'll answer every single one with honesty."

Her eyes run over my face as she considers my offer. I know it's late. The thirty minutes she granted me ended ten minutes ago. This is when she'll flee and any chance I had of getting her back will disappear with her.

Her tongue slicks her bottom lip. "I do have a question. I want to know why that letter Briella wrote to you is covered in red specks of something that looks like..."

"Blood," I interrupt her. "That note Briella wrote me is covered in her blood. She wrote it just before her father walked into her bedroom and killed her and our unborn child."

Chapter 13

Sophia

"She was pregnant?" I try not to sound as shocked as I feel. Nicholas might have been a father right now if the mother of his child and his baby weren't taken from him. "I'm sorry."

"We had just found out that afternoon." He sits back in the chair. "We were two kids who didn't have two pennies to rub together, but we were excited."

"You didn't plan the baby?"

His mouth curves. "I was in college. Briella had just graduated high school the summer before. She was working to save for tuition. It was an accident."

I was an accident. My parents joked about it to some of their friends one night when they'd had too much wine. I heard the confession and the resulting laughs when I left my bedroom to get a snack. I wasn't more than ten-years-old at the time. I asked them about it the next day and as they both stuttered their way through an explanation about God's master plan for them, I knew from the expression on their faces that they were ashamed that I'd overheard.

"I asked her to marry me once we found out she was pregnant."

The confession stings even though it shouldn't. He loved her. He told me that weeks ago, and now that I know that there was a baby involved, it makes perfect sense why her picture is on display in his apartment. He lost what would have been his family that night.

"We didn't know how we'd make it happen," he continues, his voice cracking. "I was going to quit school and get a job. She thought she'd be able to take on more hours at the café she worked at. We were determined to make it all work."

"You would have made it work," I say with no hesitation. He's built an incredible life for himself. I don't doubt that his talent for writing would have emerged back then too and his family would have been well provided for.

"I wanted to." He swallows what's left of the whiskey in his glass. "I said goodbye to Briella right after dinner that night and told her I'd have a surprise for her the next day."

The conversation feels intimate in a way that makes me long to hold him. He's in pain. It's a kind of pain I've never known. "What was the surprise?"

"I never played sports in high school, so my grandfather gave me his varsity ring before he died. He was the quarterback. Tough as nails on the outside, but the most loving guy you'd ever meet on the inside."

"He sounds amazing."

"He died a year after Briella did." His face softens. "But that night when I told him she was pregnant, he fished that ring out of a trunk in a closet. He gave it to me to give to her."

It's something my own grandfather would have done too. "That's a special ring."

"I have it in my pocket almost every day." He shifts in his seat as his hand dives into the front pocket of his pants. "It's a reminder of both of them."

I look down at the tarnished ring in his palm. Most people wouldn't see the beauty in it, but I do. It represents both love and loss to Nicholas. "You treasure it."

"With my life." His hand closes around it. "I couldn't wait to give it to her, so I went to her house."

I swallow. "What happened?"

He exhales heavily. "The front door was unlocked. I called out but no one answered, so I went in."

I want to stop him because I can't conceive the horror of what he must have witnessed in that house. "Were you there when he…"

"No." His head shakes faintly. "I heard footsteps on the upper floor so I took the stairs two at a time. I saw her sister collapse with a phone in her hand."

"What about Briella?"

He looks over my shoulder toward where Shirley must be. "I went into her room. She was already gone."

"I'm so sorry." Tears well in my eyes.

"I saw the note in her hand."

God. Oh, God.

"I took it, Sophia." He leans his elbows on the table. "I took it from her hand and when I heard the sirens approaching, I left. I fucking left her and our baby there on that bed all alone."

***

"I need you to understand something." His hand brushes my neck as he helps me with my coat. "I wasn't planning on telling you any of that tonight. It just came out."

I never doubted that. It was raw and unrehearsed. The fact that his hands are still shaking now is proof of that. "I know, Nicholas."

"No one but you knows that I was in the house."

"You didn't tell your parents or the police?" I glance at Shirley. The bar is closed and she's waiting on the two of us to leave before she shuts down. I see the impatience in her expression.

"No one." He buttons his suit jacket. "I was in shock back then. By the time I could form a coherent thought, I didn't want to reopen the wound."

"So you carried that with you all this time?" I can't help but feel sympathy for that. It's one thing to lose someone you love. It's another to bear witness to their lifeless body and the aftermath of a murder of that magnitude.

"I went to therapy after college. I worked through some of it there. My writing has helped."

He writes about death. It makes more sense to me now. "I can't imagine going through something like that."

"It changes a person at their core." He picks up my clutch from the table and hands it to me. "You have to fight to find yourself again."

He's fought. He's here now, baring himself to me.

"You gave me more than thirty minutes." He reaches for my hand and slides his fingers up my wrist to the edge of my watch. "Thank you for that."

I shiver. I can't tell if that's from the cheap wine or his touch. "You're welcome."

"Can I get another thirty minutes with you sometime this year?"

I try to force back a smile, but it's useless. "I think I can fit you in on Monday evening."

"Monday as in three days from now?" His brows lift. "Are you serious?"

"Meet me back here at seven on Monday evening."

"I'll be here at six."

I laugh. "You're eager."

"You're damn right I am." He raises my hand to his lips, kissing my palm gently. "I get to see the most incredible woman in the world on Monday at seven. Life doesn't get much better than that."

Chapter 14

Sophia

"Do you think forgiveness is a virtue, Den?"
She stops in place. "I think so. Why?"

I stare at the wall of the nursery that she's
been working on for baby Firi. Today she painted it a
pale shade of blue. Last week she opted for green. "I
talked to Nicholas last night. He's been through a lot
in his life. I've been thinking about forgiveness ever
since."

"You forgave him weeks ago, Soph." She
moves the covered can of paint with the toe of her
shoe. "You've been scared. That's different than not
forgiving."

She's right. I did forgive him even if I wasn't
ready to admit it to myself. I know that he spat those
words out because he was angry. It doesn't excuse the
fact that he chose to do it though. "What if I try again
with him and he blames me for something else that
goes wrong?"

"You'll tell him to shut the hell up and think
about what he's saying." She manages a half-grin.
"Before that happens, you'll talk to him about how he
made you feel when he accused you of stealing his
manuscript. If he listens and understands, you two
have a shot. If he just wants to push it under the rug
and forget it ever happened, you need to think twice
about getting involved with him again."

Her words are my truth. I've been thinking the same thing since I talked to him at the bar. "I'm meeting him for a drink on Monday night."

She rubs her growing belly through the pink sweatshirt she's wearing. "You haven't been the same since you two broke up."

"I'm the same," I argue.

"You're not," she insists with a push of her hair behind her shoulders. "You felt safe with him and he stole that away from you."

I don't respond. I can't. She's right.

"I know it's hard for you to trust men." She edges around the subject with skill and compassion. "You let your guard down with him. Then he went and fucked that all up."

I smile. "He fucked it up royally."

"Who knew that an award-winning author could be such a dunce?"

"Tell me I'm not an idiot for even considering taking him back." I sigh.

She rests both hands on my shoulders. "If you care about him and you believe that he's genuinely sorry for what happened, I think you're safe to follow your heart."

"How did you get to be so smart?"

"I'm not smart." She laughs it off. "I know that relationships aren't cut and dry. We all make mistakes. Nicholas did. You will too. How you handle those mistakes is what defines who you are as a couple and as individuals."

"Smart." I tip my chin up. "I still say you're smart."

"I must be. I finally chose the perfect color of paint for my little boy's nursery."

***

"White or red tonight, Sophia?" Shirley holds a bottle of wine in each hand.

"Red tonight." I smile at her. She gave me a hug when I walked into Bartlett's. Nicholas was already waiting for me at the same table we shared last week.

She fills the empty glass in front of me half full. "I'd tell you to sample it, but I don't run that kind of joint. You drink what I serve and I charge a fair price."

"Deal." I give her a wink. "Nicholas is paying though."

"In that case, I should have cracked open the good stuff."

Nicholas laughs. "We'll save that for another night."

"Suit yourself, Nicky." She turns back to me. "Can I get you something to eat? I make a mean ham sandwich."

I glance around the almost empty bar. "I didn't realize you served food here."

"I don't, but I keep a loaf of bread, a package of ham and a jar of the best mustard in the state in the fridge in the back."

"It sounds delicious," I say genuinely. "I ate at home though so I'll take a rain check."

"Deal." She looks down at the tumbler in front of Nicholas. "Can I get you a refill?"

"Not right now." He tosses her a look. "We're going to talk for a bit."

"Throw me a wave if you need another."

I watch her walk away, acutely aware that Nicholas is staring at me. I'm not wearing a stitch of makeup tonight. I got home late from work and had just enough time to eat an apple and shower. I dried my hair, pulled on a black jumpsuit and boots and took off out the door.

"I was running late." I skim my fingers over my lips. "I usually never leave the house without makeup."

"You should always leave the house without makeup. You're stunning like this."

I want to tell him that he's gorgeous too. He is. He's wearing a thick charcoal colored sweater and jeans. His hair hasn't been trimmed in weeks and he's wearing his glasses tonight.

"How is work going?"

His brows pop at my generic question. "Good. I'm working on a new project and getting things lined up for the release of *Action's Cause*."

"Does it make you nervous?" I sample the wine. It's not half bad. "Does putting a new book out make you anxious?"

"Always." He rubs the pad of his thumb over the rim of his glass. "I'm exposing a piece of myself. There's a vulnerability that goes with that."

"I understand. It's the same for me with my clothing designs."

"I met Gabe for a drink on Saturday night. He told me you're killing it at Ella Kara."

"You met Gabriel for a drink?" I don't even try to hide my surprise. "Since when do the two of you hang out?"

He dips his head down. "Since I told him he could call me whenever he wanted."

"That might have been a mistake."

He gazes across the table at me. "It might have been. If it was, I can live with it. I can't live with what I did to you, Sophia. I want to make it up to you. Tell me how."

Chapter 15

Nicholas

I stop breathing when I see the look in her eye. It's pain. Clear and honest pain caused by me. I'm so fucking pissed at myself for doing what I did to her.

"I talked to my friend, Cadence, the other day about forgiveness."

Forgive my sins, Sophia. Please fucking forgive me.

"Did it help you?" I hold my breath after I ask. I pray to God her friend isn't one of those women who hold a man's transgressions against him until his heart stops beating. If I have to walk this earth for the next sixty years knowing Sophia is out there somewhere and not by my side, I'll be dead inside.

"Talking to her always helps me." She manages a small smile. "She's very logical."

"What did she say about forgiveness?"

Her grip tightens on the wine glass. "She said that I'd forgiven you weeks ago. She's right."

"You did?" I ask hoarsely.

"If I saw some of my designs on a runway at fashion week, I'd lose it." Her voice is even and measured. "I'd think twice before blaming my lover for it, but maybe that's just me."

"You're more than my lover," I subtly correct her. "What we have is more than just that."

"We have nothing if you don't trust me."

My stomach drops. She's right. A relationship can't survive without trust. "I trust you. I trust you more than anyone else in my life."

"Do you trust me enough to talk to me about what you're feeling?" Her pale blue eyes search my face. "You can't lash out at me like that again, Nicholas. If you do, I don't think I can forgive you a second time."

"I wouldn't want you to forgive me again." I take a deep breath. "I won't hurt you, Sophia. If you give me another chance, I'll get it right. I won't fuck it up."

"You hurt me so much." She pinches the bridge of her nose. "I promised myself I wouldn't cry about this. I haven't yet, but I'm so mad at you for what you did to me."

"You should be fucking pissed." I reach across the table for her hand, but I stop myself. "I need to know how I made you feel. I want to hear it all. I want you to cry. I need you to scream at me if that helps and I want you to remind me how fucking fortunate I am to know you every single day."

"I may need to talk about this in a week, or two or maybe a year from now."

A year from now? Her eye is on the future.

"Whenever you feel the need to talk about it, you tell me. I'll drop whatever I'm doing and I'll be there for you."

She takes another sip of the wine, her nose scrunching slightly as she swallows. "I'm not promising you forever. We take this slow and see where it goes."

"I'll take it however you want." I pause. "I want to be with you. You set the rules. I'll follow your lead. Whatever you need from me is yours."

"Trust." She reaches for my hand and links our fingers together. "If you don't trust me, we have nothing to build on."

I look down at our hands. "You've got that and more."

***

"Can I see you again this week?" I ask her as we stand on the sidewalk outside Bartlett's Bar. It's still early. It's nearing nine o'clock and if I had my way, I'd take Sophia home with me, but it's too soon for that.

Her mouth twists wryly. "Back here or somewhere else?"

"You want one of Shirley's ham sandwiches, don't you?" I ask dryly. "I've had one, Sophia. I'm telling you now to steer clear of that shit."

Her thumb jerks back in the direction of the door. "Shirley's heart would break in two if she heard you talking like that."

"You're right," I acquiesce with a push of my glasses up my nose. "I'm right too. You can't eat one of those sandwiches. I won't let you."

"You won't let me?" She challenges me with a quirk of her right brow. "Is that a dare?"

"No, it's a public service. I'm pretty sure I got food poisoning the last time I had one."

She sighs dramatically. "It couldn't have been all that bad. You look fine to me."

"I look fine to you?" I emphasize the word *'fine.'* "You think I'm hot, don't you?"

"You're all right." Her gaze drifts down the street at the oncoming traffic. "I can see you on Thursday night if that works for you."

Any fucking minute of any day works for me. "I'm free."

"What do you want to do?"

Fuck you until you're raw. Listen to you play the piano. Love you.

I don't say any of those things aloud. "Tell me one thing you've always wanted to do in New York that you've never done."

Her eyes search mine as if she's looking for something there. "Do you promise you won't laugh when I tell you?"

I hold my hand in the air. "Scout's honor."

"You were never a boy scout, Nicholas."

"It doesn't matter. Tell me, Sophia. Let me give you an experience you've never had before."

She bites her lip to stall a smile. "I want to go for a ride on the Staten Island Ferry."

"Consider it done."

Chapter 16

Sophia

"You look a little green." I push on his shoulder. "Did you get seasick?"

He shakes his head. "I think I was a sailor in a past life."

"Maybe a pirate," I joke. "Most likely you were forced to walk the plank."

He scratches his whisker covered jaw. "And you were a fair maiden back then too."

He's been like this all evening; completely attentive, protective and happy. I met him in front of Bartlett's Bar at six and we took an Uber to the Whitehall Terminal. He hesitated only briefly when we boarded the ferry, but once we were on the water, he relaxed.

"Are you hungry, Sophia?"

I am. I hadn't eaten after I left work. I rushed home to change into jeans and a white sweater before I pulled on my coat, gloves, and a wool cap to help ward off the cool winds that I knew would whip at us from the water.

"I could go for a ham sandwich."

"I'll ignore that." He glances down the street. We're back in mid-town Manhattan now after Nicholas ordered an Uber to pick us up from the Terminal. "I know a burger place less than a block from here."

"I know a place where the chef makes one of the best grilled cheese sandwiches I've ever had," I say quietly." There's even a baby grand piano there. I could play it while he cooks for me."

He traces his lower lip with his index finger. "You're sure?"

I am. I thought about this a lot at work today. I want to feel close to him again and although I don't know if I'll sleep with him tonight, I want to be at his apartment with him. "Absolutely."

"I'll call for another car."

"No." I stop his hand as he reaches for his phone. "Let's take the subway. It will be like the night we first met."

He swallows hard. "The best night of my life you mean."

"Play your cards right, Mark Twain, and tonight may be the best night of your life."

"I have a feeling you're right." He leans down to press his lips to my forehead. "This is already a night I'll never forget."

***

"You really do make an excellent grilled cheese sandwich." I run my finger over the last few toasted crumbs on my plate.

He eyes my lips. "I can make you another if you want."

"I'm full." I rub my stomach through the sweater I'm wearing. "I'll take another glass of sparkling water though."

"You're sure you don't want to sample the bottle of wine I bought?"

I glance at the still corked bottle sitting between us. "I have to work on one of the designs for the Ella Kara collection when I get home tonight. I need to be stone cold sober to do that."

He gets up from his chair to retrieve the sparkling water from the refrigerator. "Gabriel thinks this line may be Foster's most successful yet."

"He told you that?" I question as I watch him fill the elegant wine glass with water. "Tell me exactly what he said to you."

He smiles as he lowers himself back into his chair. "He said that he couldn't remember a designer with as much raw talent as you and he kicks himself every day that he didn't realize that sooner."

"He didn't know." I sigh. "I never told Gabriel that I was a designer."

"I know." He picks up my glass and takes a sip of the water. "Why did you keep that a secret?"

"It's simple." I close my eyes briefly and draw a deep breath. "I was scared that he wouldn't be impressed. I was worried that I'd show him and he'd tell me to focus on being an administrative assistant."

"You doubted your ability?"

"I've always known that I have an eye for fashion." I take a swallow of water. "I was confident in what I was doing but when I went to work for Gabriel, something changed."

"What changed?" He rests his elbow on the table.

"I knew that I had one chance to impress him and every time I created a new outfit, I felt I could do better. I wanted the piece I showed him to be perfect so I kept putting it off so I wouldn't be forced to face disappointment if he rejected my work."

"You blew him away." His tone is soft. "I suppose that's obvious in the offer he made to you."

"You know the details of my contract?" I suck in a deep breath.

"No," he answers quickly; decisively. "All I know is that you're running the collection for Ella Kara and Gabriel couldn't be happier."

"I'm happy too. In the fall everyone will finally see what I have to offer. I can't wait for that to happen."

Chapter 17

Sophia

I turn to look at him once I finish playing the piano. Tonight it was another piece from Chopin. I'd mastered it years ago under the guidance of my piano teacher. She'd be disappointed in my performance just now. "Did you like that?"

"How can one person be so multi-talented?" He eyes me from where he's sitting in the chair next to the piano. "You're not only a world class fashion designer, but you could join the New York Philharmonic on stage and blend in seamlessly."

I couldn't. To an untrained ear, my ability to play may seem impressive. I heard the missteps my nervous fingers made tonight. He didn't notice because he was focused on the song as a whole, not on the intricate parts like I was.

"I'm a better designer than a pianist." I scan the small table next to the chair he's in. I instantly realize the picture of him and Briella is gone.

His gaze follows mine. "I packed it away. It was time."

"You put it away because of me." It's not a question. It's a statement. "She's important to you, Nicholas. I think you should put the picture back."

He taps his knee. "Come sit with me."

I do. We're both still fully clothed and as I snuggle into his lap, I feel a sense of instant peace when his arms circle my waist.

"For a long time, I had regrets about the night she was killed."

I turn to look at his face. "Regrets? What regrets?"

"If I wouldn't have stayed with my grandfather as long as I did, I might have made it to Briella's house before she was shot." He exhales sharply. "I regret that I didn't take her with me to see my grandfather. They'd met once before that and he adored her. I wondered for a long time how different my life would have been if she hadn't been home when her father got there."

"I read some articles online about what happened." I reach to cover his hand with mine. "He killed them late at night. It sounded as if they were all already in bed."

"It was late." He nods. "She had to get up early the next morning to open the café she worked at."

I don't want to call her death fate, but he couldn't have saved her. "There wasn't anything you could have done to change what happened."

"It took me years to realize that." He pulls me tighter to him. "It took longer than that to replace the memory of her body in her bed with an image of her face while she was alive."

"That's why you kept the picture there," I whisper against the skin of his cheek. "You wanted to remember her with that smile on her face."

"Exactly. It helped."

"Put it back." I point at the table. "I think you should have it where you can see it."

"It's time to leave Briella's memory behind me, Sophia. Life moves on. Dragging the past with me won't give me the future I want."

I absorb each and every one of those words. "Sometimes it's hard to leave the past behind."

He shifts me in his lap so he can look at my face. "I want a future with you. It's time to let the past go."

I stare at his lips. He's right. "Maybe one night next week you can come over to my place."

A smile ghosts his mouth. "I'd love that. You name the day, give me the address, and I'll be there."

"I'll text you all of that once I know my schedule."

His brow furrows slightly. "No rush, Sophia. We'll do it when you're ready."

"Next week we'll do it," I say as I lean in to kiss him. "Tonight I want to enjoy every second of being here with you."

***

I reach between us and tug on the zipper of his jeans. He's already undressed me down to my pink lace panties. He feathered kisses over my breasts before his lips and tongue worked my nipples into hard, aching points.

"I want to kiss more of you, Sophia."

"You need to be naked first."

"I might come on your leg just from the sight of your body." He smiles. "You make me feel like a teenager who can't control himself."

"Is that a bad thing?" I yank his zipper down and reach in to slide my hand against his boxer covered cock. "You're hard."

"You're surprised?" He chuckles. "I'm almost always hard when I'm around you."

"Almost always?" I stare up and into his face as I move his boxers aside. My fingertips glide over his thickness.

"My dick was limp on the ferry." He inches back a step toward the bed. "I admit I got a little seasick."

"I knew it." I follow his lead and move with him before I say jokingly, "I guess my fantasy of you fucking me in a boat will never come true now."

"If you would have been wearing a skirt, I would have fingered your pussy."

I don't doubt it. His hand brushed against my ass while we stood on the deck of the ferry looking at the lights of Manhattan in the distance. "There's always next time."

"Do you want that, Sophia? Do you want me to fuck you in public?"

I still. "Do you want that?"

"I'd have a driving urge to kill any man who saw your body, who watched you come."

"Keep me to yourself, Nicholas," I whisper against the curve of his jaw. "Protect me."

"With my life." He drops to his knees, his hands circling my waist. "I'd do anything to keep you safe. I'd do anything for you."

I weave my fingers through his hair as his mouth finds my inner thigh. "Make me forget everything but you."

Chapter 18

Nicholas

I stripped after she came against my mouth. The sweetness of her was enough to almost send me over the edge. I shed my sweater and jeans in record time. My boxers hit the floor before she was on the bed, her legs spread, her beautiful pussy on display and waiting for me.

I don't know how but I sheathed my cock without blowing my load.

Now, I'm inside her sweet body, moving slowly, savoring the feeling of her clenched tightly around me.

"Nicholas," she murmurs my name against the skin of my neck. "I love when you fuck me."

I fucking love it. I'll never get enough of this heaven even if I live for eternity.

"Slow," she says through a moan.

I slow, even though it takes every ounce of willpower I have. I want to take her wildly. I want to pin her to the sheets and fuck her senseless until the bed edges against the floor and we both come hard.

I kiss her roughly, my teeth edging along her bottom lip. "I'm too hard, Sophia. You feel too fucking good."

"You can come in my mouth." Her tongue darts out. "You taste so good."

I can't respond. I have to give every ounce of concentration I have left to my cock. The greedy bastard wants to take more than he's willing to offer right now.

I fuck her slowly, painful slow strokes that arch her back off the sheets.

She moves her legs, circling them around my waist. A wicked smile covers her lips but not a word leaves her lips. It's just crazy hot sounds of lust and need that come from somewhere deep within her.

My need to fuck takes over. I up the pace, my hips grinding out circles of desire as I pump my cock into her.

She darts over the edge into an intense orgasm without warning. Her heels dig into my back. Her fingernails etch lines of hunger down my shoulders to my biceps.

I can't control myself. I bracket her body with both of my hands and fuck her hard until I release with her nipple clenched between my teeth.

***

"It felt like you bit my nipple clean off." She rubs her breast and my cock swells.

"You don't like pain?"

"Keep that thing away from me." She tilts her chin. "How can you be hard again already?"

I sweep my eyes over her perfect naked body. "Do you really have to ask?"

"I can't fuck again right now." Her hands hover over her core. "I'm exhausted. My pussy needs a time-out."

"Your pussy needs a time-out?" I repeat back as I hold her gaze. "What the fuck is a pussy time-out?"

"It's a break from a big cock." She rolls her eyes. "When you fuck me hard like that I feel like your cock is going to split me in two."

"That's not a complaint, is it?" I trace a path along her bare shoulder. "You're not saying my cock is too big for you, are you?"

"Never." She rolls on her side to face me. "You're bigger than anyone I've been with."

I smile inwardly. I like knowing that. I've never had penis envy, but I'm glad that I can give her an experience she's never had before. "You're more beautiful than anyone I've ever been with."

"How many women do you think that is?"

"Sophia." I lean in for a soft kiss. "Don't ask me that."

"It's a lot?"

I don't want to go there for obvious reasons. I've had this discussion with women before and it's never ended well. "It's not important."

"Do you wonder about the lovers I've had?"

"No," I answer brusquely. I do, but I won't admit that to her. She's never spoken of any man in her past and although I'm glad for that, it's left me wondering if there's a reason behind it. She knows about Briella but that's a unique situation. I won't go into details about any of the other women I've fucked. None of them are worth mentioning.

"I don't want to waste the time we have together reliving our pasts." I kiss her again. "I don't care about any of your experiences with other men."

Something shifts behind her eyes. "That's fair."

Maybe it is or maybe I'm an asshole for not being open minded enough to hear her tell me about the men she cared enough about to fuck. Her words before we slept together the first time never leave my mind. She needs a connection to screw. That means that every other man who has tasted her or fucked her has meant something to her. I'm not evolved enough to be open to hearing about that. I admit it.

"Is being eaten out part of a pussy time-out or will you sit on my face?"

She laughs loudly. "I need to go home to work on that design I told you about. I'll have to pass on the face sitting tonight."

"I'd say it's your loss but it's mine. I can't tempt you at all?"

She slides her lips over mine in a slow and sensual kiss. "I have to go, but I'll keep the offer in mind for the next time we see each other."

"That better be tomorrow, Sophia."

"Maybe." She grins against my mouth. "I might be busy."

"I'll call you in the morning to find out."

"I like you a lot."

I love you, Sophia. I fucking love you.

I don't say it. Instead I repeat back her words as I stare into her eyes.

Chapter 19

Sophia

"Do you think Nicholas has slept with more women than you have?"

Crew starts coughing. "I just took a drink of coffee, Sophia. Your timing is shit. Why the fuck would you ask me a question like that?"

I squint. "You're a man, Crew."

His fingers run along his jaw. "You're correct. I'll ask my question again. Why the hell would you ask me if I've fucked more women than Nick has?"

"What's it like to sleep with so many people?"

"What's it like to ignore every question your best friend asks you?"

"Cadence is my best friend, not you."

"Tell her that if you want, but you and I know the truth."

I smile. "His number is higher than mine."

"The old lady sitting behind us probably has a number higher than you. The guy with the hunch back over in the corner does too."

"You're not funny." I shake my head. "I'm serious."

"You're self-conscious." He picks up the cup of coffee in front of him. "Don't talk while I drink. This shirt cost me more than your first car."

I wait until he swallows. "What if he wakes up one day and realizes I'm boring in bed?"

His brows perk. "You're boring in bed? I wouldn't have guessed that. I pegged you as a freak."

"You're disgusting."

"Because I'm a freak in bed? Don't knock it until you've tried it."

"I'll never try it, Crew."

"The feeling is mutual, Soph. I care about you too much to cross that line."

I take comfort in that. I know that he doesn't view me that way and I'm grateful. If he did, I wouldn't be having this conversation with him. "He mentioned the idea of fucking in public."

He doesn't flinch.

"You've done that?" I whisper as I lean over the table. "Have you done that, Crew?"

"Twice this week alone."

I sip on the mug of tea I ordered. "No details please."

"I don't fuck and tell." He shoots a smile at a middle-aged woman passing our table.

"I can't do things like that." I pull on a strand of my hair. "I like him a lot and if I'm not what he wants or needs, I'd rather know now."

"You should be having this conversation with Nick," he points out. "If you can't talk to him about stuff like this, you two are doomed."

"It's not always easy for me to talk about sex," I admit on a sigh.

"Why?"

I don't answer him. I can't. It's too personal of a conversation for me to have with him.

"You don't have to tell me anything." He straightens his tie. "Talk to Nick. The guy is head over heels for you."

"Is there anything a woman would tell you that would make you not want her?"

"If I cared for that woman the way Nick cares for you, I doubt like hell there would be."

I look at him. "You're a good friend."

"I'm the best." He finishes the last swallow of coffee at the bottom of his cup. "I'm here whenever you need me."

"Don't tell Nicholas we talked about this, Crew."

"You're not going to make me pinky swear to that, are you?"

"If I asked you to, you would." I wiggle my left pinky at him.

"You're fucking right I would." He stands and leans down to kiss my forehead. "Trust in Nick. Whatever you need to tell him, he'll understand."

I nod.

"And Sophia?" He turns back just as he starts to walk away. "My number has got to be higher than Nick's and when I stop and think about all the women I've fucked it makes me feel like shit."

He doesn't give me a chance to respond before he exits the café and heads up Broadway.

***

"You're ahead of schedule with your designs." Mr. Foster stands next to me as we look at the design board I created for Ella Kara's launch. "You only have two open spots, Sophia. I'm tempted to suggest we expand the line to four more pieces, but that's pressure I'm not sure you can handle."

Apparently, the man doesn't know me very well. "I have six more in mind."

"Six?" He steps toward the white board. "Tell me about them."

"I can do better than that." I reach for my sketchpad. "I've already chosen the fabrics. I've attached a swatch to each page and you can see the notes at the bottom that explain the accessories I feel would best complement the core design elements of the pieces."

He takes the pad from my hands and skims through the pages I've dog-eared. "This is your best work to date. Are you confident you can get these completed by launch?"

I'm certain I can have them all complete by two weeks before launch, but I don't allow my cockiness to shine through. "I can, sir."

"Move ahead on this." He hands me back my sketchpad. "I'll have Sasha assign you another two assistants."

I can use the help. I'm grateful for it too. "I'll work hard on getting these done as soon as possible, sir."

"Good." He turns to face me. "I understand that you're seeing Nicholas again."

"I am." I busy myself with the piece of fabric that's currently taking up more than half of my workstation. I'll be transforming into a strapless dress. "We've been hanging out."

"Isla would like to have you both over for dinner next week if that works for you two."

It's our first official invitation as a couple. I can't help but smile. "I'll ask Nicholas when I see him. Do you have a particular evening in mind for that?"

"Wednesday," he says without hesitation.

I know the offer has a lot more to do with Nicholas than me. Mr. Foster has never invited me anywhere, but to the party he hosted to celebrate the upcoming launch of Ella Kara.

I know that they view me as the most direct path to spend time with their favorite author. I don't mind. I like the idea of socializing with the Fosters outside of work hours.

"I'll check with Nicholas and let you know."

"I look forward to getting to know you both better, Sophia."

I look forward to the look on Nicholas's face when he realizes that Isla Foster is an even bigger fan of his than her husband.

Chapter 20

Nicholas

My hands roam Sophia's body, stopping to grab her ass. I pull her closer to me. "When I'm not with you, I think about this. Do you know how hard it is to get any work done when your girlfriend has an ass like this?"

"I can't say that I do." She giggles, her breath teasing my cheek. "It's freezing in here. Can't we get under the covers?"

"No," I answer quickly. "I want to see your body. I could stare at it all day."

"It feels like you have been."

"You only got here an hour ago." I know that for a fact. I waited all day for her to arrive. She came over to my place straight from work. I ordered food so that she'd have sustenance and so that I could get the dinner part over with early. My plan all along was to feast on her for the evening. That was postponed when she took a seat at the piano and played two pieces by Schumann.

"Did you think about me today?"

I laugh at the absolute absurdity of the question. "Want do you think?"

"I think the answer is *yes*."

I kiss the sweet smelling skin near her collarbone. "It's *yes*. I think about you most of the time."

"I think about you sometimes too." She sighs when my lips move lower.

"Just sometimes?" I ask before I roll her right nipple between two of my fingers.

"That feels so good," she murmurs. "And *yes*, Nicholas, just sometimes."

She's teasing me. I hear it in the tone of her voice. "Tell me what you want me to do to you."

Her entire body stills. "I want you to fuck me."

The lights in my bedroom are dimmed, but I still see the blush that creeps up her chest and onto her neck and face. "Say it again."

"I want you to fuck me," she whispers.

I move so I'm perched above her. "That's the sexiest thing I've ever heard."

"It's not."

"It is." I stare down at her mouth. "Tell me you like my cock, Sophia."

Her tongue darts out over her bottom lip. "I do like it."

"Say it. Say you like how my cock feels when I'm fucking you."

"If you know it already, why do I have to say it?"

My cock swells even more. "I want to be rock hard when I take your cunt."

Her eyes drop and a small moan escapes her throat. "You say things no man has ever said to me before."

"Every man you've been with in the past is an absolute idiot."

Her eyes widen as she shifts her legs underneath me. "You said you didn't want to talk about them."

"I don't." I kiss her softly. "I just know that any man who has been inside of you knows what a gift that is. How a man walks away from that is beyond me."

"You walked away from me."

She's right. I did. I regretted it instantly and it had little to do with the way her pussy grips me when I'm fucking her. It had nothing to do with the taste of her or the way she screams my name. It had everything to do with what I feel inside for her. "That was temporary insanity, Sophia. It won't happen again."

"You can't say that for certain." Her fingers run over my chest. "You don't know what will happen between us in the future."

"I'm not leaving you again." I stare into her eyes. "You gave me a second chance. There's no way in hell that I'm fucking that up."

"You think we'll be together for a while then?"

Forever, Sophia. I think we'll be together forever because if we're not, my lungs will never fill with enough oxygen again. You give me life. You make me see the potential of tomorrow.

"Do you want to be with me in the future?" I ask her. "Tell me what your future looks like."

"I feel safe and loved."

"By me?" I ask as I kiss her temple. "Tell me that it's me that you see in your future."

"Only you," she whispers on a sigh. "You're the only man I see in my future."

I love you. I mouth the words against her cheek before I slide my hand down her body and along the seam of her pussy.

"Make me come with your fingers." She opens her legs for me.

I circle her swollen clit with the pad of my thumb. "I'll make you come like this if you promise me I can fuck you raw in the shower."

Her hips circle in a slow sensual dance. "How can I say *no* to that?"

I kiss her, my tongue stroking the inside of her lips as I strum a beat over her clit and drive her to the edge of her first orgasm of the night.

***

"Nicholas!" She screams my name as I wrap both her thighs around my waist. "It's too much."

"It's never enough," I pant between thrusts. I've got her in my arms, her back against the tiled wall of my shower as hot water beats down on us.

I lapped at her pussy after she came against my lips. Then I kissed her softly, knowing that she was experiencing the same taste of her that I had.

After that, I carried her to the shower. She dropped to her knees to take me in her mouth, but I yanked her back up after less than two minutes. Coming all over her face is something I crave but blowing my load anywhere but inside of her isn't happening right now.

I sheathed my aching cock, cursing the fact that I had to. I want inside of her with nothing on. I want to feel the tight walls of her pussy gripping me like a vise. I need that but I know she's not ready for that step. I don't fucking blame her. There are risks that come with sex without a condom.

Once I turned the water on, she melted into my arms. Her damp hair clung to the side of her face, veiling the sheen that had overtaken her skin when she came earlier.

Now, as I fuck her with long easy strokes, she whimpers against me.

I want her to come again before I do, so I up the tempo.

Her lips press a kiss to my jaw as every thrust takes me deeper. "Nicholas…"

The only thing that follows my name is a low moan as she comes in sweet surrender before I fuck her to my own release.

Chapter 21

Sophia

"Are you busy next Wednesday?" I towel dry my hair. "Gabriel invited us for dinner at his place."

"Did he?" He pulls on a pair of black sweatpants. "I'd love to go. Are you good with that?"

I am. I'm actually looking forward to it. I haven't had a chance to see Nicholas and Gabriel together since they've become friends. I miss Isla too. When I was Gabriel's assistant, she'd stop in to see him at least a few times a week. Now that I'm in the design department, I don't get a chance to chat with her.

"I think we'll have a good time."

"I know we will." He hangs up the towel he used to dry my body after our shower. "We should bring something. Wine or flowers, maybe?"

"I think the fact that you're going to be there is the only gift they need," I joke.

He rolls his eyes, but smiles. "Gabriel's gotten over the fact that I'm Nicholas Wolf."

"You haven't met Isla yet." I bite my lower lip. "She's a bigger fan than Gabriel. Expect to be the center of attention at that dinner."

"I may be the center of attention for her, but you'll have my attention for the entire evening."

I know that he's desperate to make up for what happened between us at Hibiscus, but I take every word he says to me now at face value. I've never felt as cherished by a man as I do by him.

I'm tempted to ask if I can stay the night, but I want to present the finished sample of one of my new designs for Ella Kara to Sasha tomorrow morning. "I need to get home. I have a lot of work to do."

"I can take you." He pats his bare chest. "I just need to throw on a coat and some shoes and I'm good to go."

Panic washes over me. I shouldn't feel like this. He's safe. "It's cold out. I can manage to get home on my own."

His eyes scan my face, stopping on my kiss-swollen lips. "Trust is a two-way street, Sophia."

I know it is. I've told myself that over-and-over again the last few weeks. He broke my trust in him and he's been working overtime to rebuild it. "I trust you."

"Do you have a roommate?" He leans his hip against the bathroom counter.

"No," I answer quickly, toying with the belt of the white robe he wrapped me in after I stepped out into the cool bathroom from the heated shower. "I live alone."

"You don't live at work, do you?"

"Sometimes it feels that way," I say to avoid what I should be saying. "I have an apartment. It actually belongs to Cadence. I was her roommate before she moved in with Tyler."

"Are you a hoarder?" There's amusement in his tone. I know he's trying to lighten the mood but it's not helping. "If I come over will you have hundreds of empty take-out containers covering every inch of available space?"

"Only on the nights when I watch Netflix with Cadence."

"Tell me why, Sophia." He stalks toward me. "Tell me why I can't come to your place."

"I don't want to have this discussion in a bathroom," I stall. "And it's late. We should talk about this another time."

He reaches for my hand. "Come with me."

I have no choice. I follow him in silence, the entire time my heart pounding so hard it feels like the wall of my chest will split open.

He stops when we near the piano bench. "Sit."

I do. I lower myself onto the bench, carefully tucking the long robe around my legs. He pulls the chair next to the piano along the floor until it's right in front of me. When he sits down, his knees touch mine.

"I want to understand the hesitation." He cradles both of my hands in his. "Trust me enough to tell me what's going on."

Cadence is the only person in New York City who knows. I thought I could leave my past back in Florida but that's proven impossible. "Do you remember that call I took when we were at the hotel?"

He nods his head briskly. "The day we went up to Mrs. Foster's suite and ate a fantastic burger on her dime?"

"Yes." I lower my eyes to our hands.

"Who called?"

"A lawyer." My hands start to shake but he quiets them. His thumbs trace small circles on my palms.

"Your lawyer?" His voice is as gentle as his touch. He's guiding me toward a confession. He deserves it. I kept justifying in my mind that I was right to not share this part of my life with him after what happened between us at Hibiscus. I was using his mistake to shelter my secret. It was wrong. I see that now. He wants to care for me and he can't fully do that if he doesn't understand my hesitation to take him to my place.

"No." I skip past the explanation of who the woman was who called me that night. "Something happened when I was living in Florida. I need to tell you about that."

Our eyes catch. I see understanding in his. I'm sure he sees reluctance in mine. "Take it as slowly as you need to. I'm not going anywhere."

I want to go. I want to bolt and pretend that what happened was all a bad dream. I don't want him to look at me any differently than he has up to this point. I don't want his touch to become tentative and guarded out of fear that I'll buckle from the pain of my past. "It was a long time ago. It happened back in Florida."

He doesn't flinch. The statement is so general that I expected a deluge of questions to follow.

"It was during my first year of college. I wanted the full experience so I rented an apartment off campus."

"I can understand that."

Our eyes catch. "I was dating a man. A boy, I guess. We were the same age."

His jaw tightens. "Did he hurt you?"

That's a hard question to answer. Franco never raised a hand to me. He was as kind as anyone I'd ever met, but that doesn't mean he wasn't dangerous. "I broke up with him after we slept together a few times. It wasn't good. I didn't feel anything for him and the experience left me with so much regret."

"He didn't take it well?"

I shake my head. "He was angry, sad, the whole gamut of emotions that come with a bad break-up. He tried to get me back for months after that."

"You held strong though?" He runs a hand down his bare chest. It's a thoughtless gesture on his part but it stirs something within me. He's muscular and firm. He could probably pummel Franco to near death with his bare hands.

I shake off the thought. "I didn't want to be with him. I told him that over and over but he wouldn't stop bothering me. He'd follow me everywhere, send me flowers and gifts. He even showed up at my parent's house in a tuxedo asking for their permission to marry me."

"He sounds unstable." He lets out a deep breath. "Did you speak to the police about him?"

"Dozens of times." I rub my temple. "I took out so many restraining orders that I lost count. He was arrested just as many times."

"He was stalking you." It's a clear statement. "What an asshole."

"Eventually he went to jail. It had nothing to do with me. He was convicted of tax evasion." I sigh wishing that was the end of the story. "He got out early a few months ago."

"Has he contacted you since?"

I nod. "I saw him once on the sidewalk outside Foster Enterprises. I ran to the security guard who is always in the lobby and Franco disappeared around the corner. I called the police then."

"So there's a restraining order now? It's valid in New York?"

I scrub my hand over my face. "Yes and he's back in Florida now."

"How can you be sure?" He taps my knee with his fingers. "Do you have someone trailing him?"

"My dad," I chuckle. "My dad knows where Franco works. He keeps an eye on the place and lets me know when he's not around."

"I can have someone shadow you, Sophia. I can do it myself if need be. I don't want this guy getting close to you again."

I should tell him that I doubt like hell that Franco would ever raise a hand to me but it's impossible to predict what someone who is emotionally unstable will do. "I'm fine. As long as I know where he is I feel safe."

"He knows you work at Foster," he says quietly. "Does the fucker know where you live?"

I take a deep breath. This is it. "No. Only a handful of people know where I actually live and I want you to be one of them."

Chapter 22

Nicholas

If given the chance I'd find the son of bitch who has put this fear in Sophia, and I'd steal his life from him. Short of that, I'd get my lawyer to drum up some charge that would send his ass back to jail for good.

"When I first got to New York I stayed in a rundown motel in Queens." She moves her legs slightly, causing her ass to shift on the chair. "After I moved in with Cadence, I asked the woman who owned the motel if I could still use it as a mailing address. She said it was fine as long as I gave her a twenty dollar bill every month, so I do. When I have mail, she calls me and I go down and pick it up."

"Did he ever show up there?"

"Once." She raises her index finger in the air. "I found out about it when I picked up my mail. They told him I'd moved out months before. He waited in their parking lot in a rental car for days to confirm that."

"You don't think he's followed you home from Foster?"

"No." Her back straightens. "Whenever I know he's left Florida, I take extra precautions. My friend Dexie usually sends a car for me those days and I leave out Foster's service entrance and spend the night with her."

"But you said you saw him outside Foster Enterprises one day? Did your father not realize he'd left Florida?"

"My dad had a heart attack." Her voice is calm, her expression as well. "It was then."

"I want his name, Sophia. If you won't let me hire someone to shadow you, I'll have someone trail him."

I want that. It would give me a level of peace I've craved. It would also put me in his debt. "We can talk about that."

"We will." He rubs my calf. "Tell me why you were speaking to a lawyer about all of this."

"It was the lead prosecutor on the case." I smile slightly. "She's a good person and we've kept in touch. She wants to help, but her hands are tied. That day she called when we were at the hotel, she was checking in to make sure I was all right."

I like knowing that someone in Florida's legal system has her back. It's not enough though. I can't stomach the thought of her walking down a street in this city alone now. "I'm glad to hear that. A case like this has to be frustrating for someone out to do the right thing."

"I'm sorry I didn't let you come to my place." She leans forward, dragging her hand along the sash of the robe. "I've always thought that the fewer people who know where I live, the better."

It's a painful pill to swallow, but I get it. She's been trying to protect herself from a monster who can't let her go.

"I want to come to your place, Sophia. I want to have a friend of mine install an alarm system for you."

"I have one." She nods. "Cadence had it put in before I moved in. She said it's the best of the best."

Regardless of cost, it's still not enough to grant me peace of mind. "I'll have a look at it when I come over."

She glances back at the green flashing light on the security panel by my front door. "You're an expert."

"I have that to protect material things. Your security system has to protect you. It needs to do its job."

"It does." She slides closer to me. "Will you take me home now, Nicholas?"

When I thought about seeing her place for the first time, I envisioned a round of fucking to christen it under my touch. That's not going to happen tonight. I'll follow her lead but all I want is to hold her in my arms for the rest of her life. "I'll call for a car."

"Let's take the subway." Her face brightens with a smile. "I love taking the subway with you."

She likes melding into the crowd. It's her way of staying invisible. "I'm game as long as you promise to hold my hand."

She reaches to grab my left hand. "I promise I'll hold tight and never let go."

***

"I own the building she lives in." Crew looks out his office window at the skyline of Manhattan. "I haven't told her that because she'd flip out. Sophia thinks I'm one of those arrogant billionaires who own half this city."

"You are one of those arrogant billionaires who own half the city." I chuckle.

"There's a security guard at the door of her building at all times. I'll speak to the manager of the security team and fill him in on this dick that's stalking her. They'll keep an eye out for him. Give me his name."

"Franco Abano. I sent you an email on my way here with all the details Sophia gave me. His work history, all the shit like that is in there."

"Good. Let's talk about this Ella Kara thing she's got going on."

After Sophia had taken me to her apartment last night, I asked her if Crew knew about Franco. She told me he didn't, but she said she'd be fine with me filling him in. I did just that as I rode the subway back to my place after kissing her goodnight. He was almost as alarmed as I was although I could tell he wasn't alone. He suggested I meet him at his office first thing this morning to discuss what steps I should be taking to protect Sophia. I would have asked Sebastian for his advice, but he's deep in a case right now.

I spent most of last night thinking about Ella Kara. Sophia's name and face are going to be splashed across every fashion magazine in the country come fall. Even though Franco already knows she's based in New York, it gives him insight into where she'll be at certain times. She's the brand, so she'll be expected to be on stage when the collection debuts at New York Fashion Week. That makes her vulnerable in a way I can't accept.

"I'll hire someone to shadow her." My gaze shifts from the view of the city to his face. "You must have people you use. Give me a name."

"Run this by her first, Nick." His fingers graze over the screen of his phone. "Give her a chance to have a say in this. She's proud. She'll be pissed if you hire someone to protect her without her input."

He's right. Sophia insisted last night before I left that she was fine. I can't take steps to deal with this without speaking to her first. "I appreciate your help with this, Crew."

"Sophia's like a sister to me. I love her almost as much as I love Lark. I'd do anything to keep Lark safe. It's the same for Sophia in my mind."

I know how much his younger sister means to him. He'd step in front of a bus for her. "I'll talk to Sophia and then I'll get moving on security for the launch of Ella Kara."

"Or I'll go down to Florida and talk to Franco."

I chuckle." Talk or beat the shit out of?"

"Whatever works, my friend. If he doesn't back off, I'll have someone down there pay him a visit."

"No need." I stand, shoving my chair back. "If it comes to that, I'll take care of it myself."

Chapter 23

Sophia

"You've done excellent work on this collection, Sophia." Sasha holds up the latest sample I created. It's a fitted dress with an embroidered bodice and a slit up the back of the skirt. "I'm impressed with this one in particular. I think we should have one of our team make a mock-up in red."

I'd considered that before I'd taken hours out of my life to make it in black. "That's fine. We can show both to Gabriel."

"We will." Her fingers play with the pearl bracelet on her arm. "I have to admit; I was hesitant when Gabriel first suggested this idea."

"The idea of the Ella Kara label bearing my name?" I've expected this conversation for weeks. Sasha has held a pivotal position within the design department of Foster Enterprises for years. She's nurtured the careers of many aspiring designers and has watched several, including Evlin Dawn, branch out and establish collections of their own. It has to sting that I was given this opportunity and not her.

"I knew you had talent." She touches my forearm, her fingers gentle. "We had a discussion more than a year ago when I came up to Gabriel's office. Do you recall?"

I would have felt embarrassed to have this conversation a few months ago, but not now. I've proven my worth to her and to everyone who has been working in this department for years. "I criticized your choices in the winter line last year."

She straightens, her hands going to her hips. "I questioned myself for months about those choices. I debated them, changed them, and then changed them back."

It's the first I've heard of it. I assumed she was confident in the pieces she'd chosen. Her demeanor during that conversation suggested as much.

"I knew that day that you had a special sense about you." She turns to stare at the white board where I've sketched each piece that I'm including in Ella Kara's initial offering. "I mentioned it to Gabriel. He told me it was expected that you'd have an opinion since you worked in the industry as an assistant."

I'm not surprised that Mr. Foster viewed it that way. I was there to cater to him. That's what the man was paying me for. My value beyond that wasn't apparent. "He wasn't aware that I was a designer back then."

"None of us were." She moves to face me again. "I'll retire in the next year or two, Sophia. I'm glad I didn't before now. Working with you on this has been one of the highlights of my career."

I swallow back the flood of emotion I feel. "You can't know how much your words mean to me. I've idolized you for a very long time."

"Not that long." She taps the tip of my nose with her finger. "You've admired me for a few years, dear. It's been just a few years."

I smile at the reminder not to bring up her age. "Yes, you're right. It's been a few years and having the chance to work with you has made me a better designer. "

***

"You told Nicholas about Franco?" Cadence stands in the lobby of my apartment building. "Things must be serious."

I'd called her on my lunch break to fill her in. I could tell she was surprised, but I had no idea it would shock her enough to lure her down to my building at the end of the day. "I hadn't brought him here yet. I thought he deserved an explanation."

I'm tempted to let her respond, but I don't. I keep talking. "Why are you here? I thought you were meeting Tyler for dinner at Nova tonight."

"He bailed." She tries to fasten a button in the middle of her coat but it's never going to happen. Her belly has popped and the coat is at least two sizes too small now. "I thought we could hang out and catch up on our Netflix show."

I hate to turn her away. Cadence has always been there for me but this dinner at Mr. Foster's is exactly what I need tonight. I haven't seen Nicholas in days. I've been too busy with the impending Ella Kara launch and he's been immersed in the novel he's writing. Our only communication has been a few calls and text messages.

"I'm sorry, Den. I have plans. I'm going to Mr. Foster's apartment for dinner tonight."

"You're what?" Her expression immediately brightens. "That's a big deal, Soph. You're rubbing elbows with Manhattan's elite."

"I'm not," I scoff as I loop my arm through hers. "Come upstairs and we can talk while I get ready."

"Do you have any chocolate chip cookies?"

"I think so." I stab the elevator call button. "Do you have a craving?"

Tipping her chin, she looks down at me. "I do. Please tell me you have goat cheese."

I step back as several people exit the elevator. "You're not planning on combining those two things, are you?"

"I'm going to make a chocolate chip, goat cheese sandwich while you get ready for your fancy dinner."

I move forward onto the elevator once it's cleared. "I just lost my appetite."

Chapter 24

Nicholas

"Thank you for letting me pick you up at your place."

Her gaze shifts from the back of the driver's head to my face. We're in the backseat of a sedan, part of the fleet from the car service I use on occasion. I'm apt at getting around the city via Uber or public transportation but tonight is special. I knew Sophia would wear something memorable; something that deserved a heated seat and a comfortable headrest.

She looks breathtaking. Her dress is a deep royal blue, her heels nude. She's left her hair down and the entire image is mesmerizing. If this dinner weren't as important to her as I know it is, I'd have taken her to her bedroom as soon as I arrived at her place.

"We can go back there after dinner." Her eyebrows wiggle. "I have something to show you."

I inch my hand up her thigh, pushing the fabric of her dress with it. "Do you keep it under here?"

Her gaze falls on my hand. "Do you want to touch me now?"

I want to fuck her now. I have a condom in the inner pocket of my suit jacket. All I need to do is tell the driver to circle the park while I pull Sophia onto my lap and fuck her sweet body until sweat dots her upper deep red lip. The only separation between the driver and us would be a thin plastic partition.

"I'd fuck you now if you'd agree to it."

She inches her ass on the seat. "Have you done that before? Have you screwed a woman in the back of a car like this?"

She was a fan, drunk on the attention I gave her at a book signing. It was an early summer evening in a car that was taking me to the airport in Dallas. I invited her along for the ride and fucked her while her face was pressed against the sticky fake leather of the seat. I never knew her name.

"Don't ask me that."

"I'll take that as a *yes*." She raises the corner of her mouth in a challenge. "Where else have you had sex?"

"Sophia." My tone is low. It's a warning. "We agreed that we wouldn't discuss past lovers."

I wait for her to bring up the fact that I now know every detail about the life of one of her former boyfriends, Franco Abano.

"We're adults." She checks her watch. "We won't be at Gabriel's for at least ten minutes so let's talk about what we did and didn't like with our past lovers."

I don't want to. I can't imagine a scenario where discussing the intimate details of sex with another woman will end well. Sophia has a jealous streak whether she'll attest to it or not. It's what lured her down from the balcony at Veil East. She saw me talking to Penny. She envisioned the two of us fucking and she decided to put a stop to it. It's as simple as that.

"I won't discuss the women I've slept with, Sophia. That's all in my past."

She huffs. "You don't have to tell me their names or how you rate them. I'm asking what you liked doing with them."

Everything she can imagine and more. "Where is this coming from?"

Her eyes skim over the front of my pants before they level on my face. "You like having sex in places where you can get caught."

"Do I?" I bark out a laugh. "I'm an exhibitionist now?"

"You said you'd fuck me on the Ferry and just now you wanted to fuck me in this car. You have a condom in your pocket, don't you?"

I won't lie to her. "I do."

"I've never done those things." She lowers her voice to a whisper. "I don't know if I ever could."

Restless, I move to touch her hand, but she pulls it back. "Sophia, don't assume anything about me."

"If you need a woman in your life who will fuck you in the middle of the day on the Brooklyn Bridge, I'm not her."

"I need you." I lean forward on the seat so I can look at her directly. "If I have a driving need to fuck in public it's because I crave you constantly. I want you every second of the day."

The only response I get is silence.

"For the record, anything I've ever done with a woman in my life isn't even a memory worth holding onto at this point. I want you. I want us to be together, alone when we make love." I push her hair behind her ear to get a better view of her profile. "I cherish you, Sophia. That condom is for later. You told me you hadn't allowed many people into your apartment, so I assumed you wouldn't have protection there."

"If we never have sex in a public place, you're all right with that?"

I am. The few times I've done it has been exciting but they've been nothing compared to being with her. "Completely."

Her shoulders ease back into the seat. "That's the last time we'll talk about the past."

It's not. At some point, we need to have a discussion about that fucked up asshole, Franco Abano. It's just not happening tonight.

***

Cruel irony is a part of life that no one can prepare for. As I walked into the foyer of Gabriel Foster's lavish penthouse, my mind was focused on one person. A man from Sophia's past. I was reading a text from Crew about Franco Abano when I heard a familiar voice from across the room.

My past was standing in the center of a large living area with a glass of wine in her hand and a tall, bearded man by her side. Her long red hair looked just as it did that day eight years ago when I ran past her at the top of the staircase of her home in search of her sister.

Lilly Parker, Briella's sibling, is here.

We haven't spoken since the joint funeral where she was forced to say goodbye to her sister, her two brothers and her mother. We never mentioned her father in our conversations but I knew that she mourned the loss of him too. It wasn't the loss of his life but the loss of the trust she had in him.

"Lilly," I whisper her name knowing she can't hear me. Sophia does.

"That's Briella's sister," she says it matter-of-factly as if the pain that bonds Lilly and I doesn't exist. It's the reason we've never sought each other out. I can't look at her and not see Briella in the contour of her jaw or the color of her eyes. She can't look at me and not see the promise of the future that her sister lost.

"Sophia." A petite, obviously pregnant woman approaches us. "This must be Nicholas."

My eyes dart to the other room and Lilly. She's still so engrossed in her conversation that she doesn't notice our presence.

Sophia reaches to hug the woman. "Isla, this is Nicholas Wolf."

Isla Foster's face immediately blushes red. "I'm your biggest fan. I know people say that to you every single day but they're all liars. I have read every book you've ever written at least nine times.""I'm flattered," I say as I look at her face. She's pretty, young, her eyes a shade of blue similar to Sophia's.

"I can get you a drink." She grabs my hand. "I bought the brand of scotch Deacon drinks in *Burden's Proof*. I thought it must be a shout-out to your favorite. "

It was a subtly placed sponsor ad meant to drum up business for a failing liquor company. That was the brainchild of Cheyenne. I have no idea if their sales increased. I doubt it since they haven't contacted us for a new deal. "That'll be fine."

Sophia shoots me a look. "Can you give us a minute, Isla? I have to ask Nicholas something."

Disappointment wages war with confusion on her face. "I'll be in the kitchen getting a scotch and a glass of red wine for you, Sophia."

When she's finally out of earshot, Sophia tugs on the lapels of my suit jacket, so I turn until my back is to Lilly. "We can leave, Nicholas. If you don't want to talk to her, we can go."

I've run from my past for eight years. I've avoided Lilly at social gatherings. On the anniversary of Briella's death, I've always stayed offline. There are too many articles, tributes and remembrances to the family who lost their lives that day.

Lilly's face is always in the midst of it all. The organ donation app she developed is dedicated to the family she lost. She's turned her tragedy into a triumph. She's helped thousands of people find an organ match. Beyond that, she's been instrumental in introducing organ recipients their donor families. Stories of those meetings have punctuated daytime television for the past two years.

I feel a faint tap on my shoulder and I know. I fucking know that I can't run now.

Sophia inches to the side so she can look behind me. I won't let her bear the brunt of this for me. I have to face Lilly, so I do.

I turn on my heel and look right at her. Her eyes fill with tears. "Nick. It is you."

"Lilly." I hold out my arms praying she'll hug me.

She moves forward quickly, her arms circling me. "I thought I'd never see you again."

Chapter 25

Sophia

I sat through dinner quietly watching Nicholas as the weight of the world slowly left his shoulders. We haven't spoken at length about what his relationship with Lilly was like after her sister's death but judging by what I saw tonight; they've turned a corner.

Isla met Lilly at a mom and baby swimming lesson late last year. They hit it off immediately and have since become friends. When Gabriel suggested to her that they host a dinner party, she thought Lilly and her husband Clive would be excited to meet Nicholas because of his notoriety. She had no idea about the history of Lilly and Nicholas. Gabriel was just as stunned when Lilly described their unique bond.

"Tonight went well." Nicholas reaches for my hand. We've been in the car for more than five minutes and neither of us has said a word to the other. He's been deep in thought and I haven't wanted to interrupt that. "I'll see her for lunch in a week or two. I'd like you to be there."

It's an invitation I want to refuse, but I won't. If he wants me by his side, I'll do it. "I can make it."

"Sasha will let you out of the design dungeon for an hour or two?"

I lean against his shoulder as the driver maneuvers the streets of Manhattan toward my apartment. "It's not a dungeon. I love being there."

He squeezes my bare knee. "It's where you belong."

I know he's right. I only spoke to Gabriel briefly about the upcoming exclusive viewing event we have planned for some of Foster Enterprises employees. There won't be more than a dozen people there, but their opinion matters to Gabriel and if I can impress them, the anxiety that has haunted his expression for weeks will ease.

Launching a new line is a monumental and risky undertaking. Doing it with a new designer at the helm comes with even more trepidation.

"I have to sleep sometimes," I joke segueing into the question I've been longing to ask all night. "I wouldn't mind having someone on the other side of the bed tonight."

The raw need in his eyes tells me everything I need to know before he even says a word. "I'll stay."

"Don't expect me to cook you breakfast, Nicholas."

"I'll handle that." He cups my cheek in his hand. "I'll take care of you tonight and tomorrow morning too."

***

I reach between us and grab his cock, cradling it in my palm. It's semi-hard which is surprising. I went to take a shower, unsure of whether his plan was to fuck or not. His night has been emotional and when he yawned twice on the way back to my apartment, I resigned myself to the fact that he may want to hold me and take comfort in my presence. I didn't assume that we'd make love, but now, I'm not so sure.

"You fell asleep," I whisper against his whisker covered jaw. "You were snoring when I came back in from the shower."

"Bullshit," he growls. "I don't snore."

"Next time I'll record it on my phone."

"You would do that to me, wouldn't you?" His hands find my ass, tugging me closer to his nude body.

"I liked watching you sleep."

"Why?" He inhales deeply. "You smell good. Is that soap or you?"

"Both." I nuzzle closer still. "You look peaceful when you sleep. It's like all those characters that run around in your mind all day have left."

"You think I have characters running around in my mind?"

I push his hardening cock against my bare core. "I see it behind your eyes. You're always plotting. Your mind never shuts down."

"It can't." He circles his hips. "I have too many stories to tell."

"Tell me a story now." I move my legs to gain better access, rubbing his erection against my clit.

"Once upon a time, there was a woman…"

I inch closer still, taking what I can from him. "Keep talking."

"Keep doing what you're doing." He groans deeply. "Can you get off like this?"

I murmur a sound that I'm sure sounds like a *yes* to him.

"Once upon a time this very good-looking guy with a huge cock met a woman on the subway."

"So this isn't about you?" I throw my head back, enjoying the sensation of the approaching orgasm.

"It's about me." He presses his lips to my neck. "The woman he met was beautiful, smart and he wanted her the second he saw her."

"So he wrote out an invitation to lunch in his own book," I continue even though I'm losing focus on anything but what I'm doing to myself with his cock. "It was a weak move."

"She secretly liked how ballsy he was."

"No, she didn't," I whimper.

He reaches down to grab his cock, his hand circling mine. "She did. She wanted him from the start. She knew he was different. She knew he was the one."

"The one?" I arch my back as the orgasm inches up on me. "What one?"

His hand grabs my ass, tugging me closer still until my clit is pressed so tightly against the side of his cock that I hit the cliff and tumble over.

"The one who loves her." His words weave into my moan as we both grasp for breath.

Chapter 26

Nicholas

"Are you going to ignore what I said to you?" I rub her shoulder as I watch her pretend to sleep. "You're a shit liar and an even worse actress, Sophia."

"I'm not acting," Her eyes stay closed. "I'm not ignoring anything."

"I told you I love you."

She rests her forehead against my chin. "I know, Nicholas. I heard it."

Begging a woman to tell me she loves me isn't something I'm willing to do. "I meant it."

"It was a heated moment." Her eyes finally open and search my face. "You were aroused. I was too. People say things when that happens."

"They say things like *fuck, that's good* or *more*, or *deeper*."

"There are other things they say too." She sighs. "You might not have really meant it."

"Bullshit," I blurt out. "I told you I love you because I do."

Her bottom lip quivers but she stills it with her teeth. "Wait until tomorrow and see if you still feel the same way."

"What the fuck is going to change between now and then?" I pull her closer.

She searches my eyes. "I don't want you to say things to me that you don't mean."

"I mean it, Sophia."

"How can you be sure?" Her voice is tinged with fear. "If you say those words to me, I need to know you mean them. You can't take them back."

Fuck me. This woman. She's scared to hand her heart over to me.

I tilt her head back, so I can look into her eyes. "Don't mistake wheat I'm feeling, Sophia. This is real. All of it."

"I want to believe you," she whispers into the still air between us. "I want to because my heart wants to say the same thing to you."

"Tell me. Say it."

Her lips part and then close, then part before she speaks. "I love you, Nicholas. Please never hurt me."

***

"Losing him is not acceptable." I feel my jaw tick. "I told you that I want you on Franco twenty-four, seven. If he's headed to New York right now, you better be prepared to find another career. I guarantee that you'll never work another security job as long as you live."

I slam my phone on the desk in my office. The security detail Crew connected me with in Florida lost sight of Franco Abano two hours ago. There's no way in hell he'd be in New York at this point. If he's coming here to harass Sophia, I'll make certain he understands that he'll need to get through me first.

"Who are you going all bad cop on right now?" Cheyenne walks in with a paper coffee cup in each hand. "You were running through a scene out loud, weren't you? I think you should rewrite it. It didn't sound believable at all to me."

I shake my head as I reach for one of the cups. "Why the coffee? Come to think of it, why are you here at all? I gave you the week off."

"It's good to see you too, Nick."

I manage a smile. I had planned on spending the day immersed in my newest manuscript. The ordeal with Joe set me back months. I have a deadline in two weeks that I'm struggling to meet.

I left Sophia's apartment this morning with her. As soon as I got back to my place, I was working until the security guy from Florida fucked up my entire day.

"What do you want, Cheyenne?" I ask, knowing she'll overlook my bluntness. She's used to it and I pay her well enough that she can ignore it. "I want that key back that I gave you when you crashed here when I took off for Brazil."

"You're never getting that key back." She blows on the steaming coffee. "I need access to you at all times."

"I'll change the locks."

"You wouldn't." She plops herself down on the weathered leather chair next to my desk. "We have a date next Tuesday night."

"I'm committed to Sophia." I wink at her. I know she'll have questions, but I'll answer every one. Sophia is an important part of my life now and my publicist needs to realize that. My book tours have to accommodate time back here in New York every two weeks. I refuse to be away from Sophia for longer than that.

"You're getting married?" Her eyes light up. "Can I be your best person?"

"If I were getting married, which I'm not, I'd choose one of my brothers as my best man. I doubt you'd even make it onto the guest list."

"You're an asshole." Her smile contradicts the bite in the words. "So if you're committed to her, but not getting married, what exactly does that mean?"

"I love her," I say with conviction. "I'm in love with her."

"Who would have thought back on that night that your manuscript went viral that we'd be having this discussion?"

"You never know what's on the horizon." I lean back in my chair. "Now, explain what you and I have going on next Tuesday night."

Chapter 27

Sophia

"You want me to go with you to a school with you so I can read books out loud?" I shudder at the thought. "Public speaking isn't my thing, Nicholas."

"You're the designer behind Ella Kara, Sophia." He places both of his hands on my shoulders. "You don't think you're going to have to do interviews or make an announcement on launch day?"

I scan his face. "Shit. Holy shit. I hadn't thought of that."

He shakes his head and laughs. "It's a middle school, Sophia. They're hosting a career night. I'm one of the feature speakers and part of the agreement was that I'd stay and read a few chapters of *Action's Cause*."

"Is that book even appropriate for a bunch of kids that age?" I eye him suspiciously. "It's graphic, isn't it?"

"I guarantee you that the video games they play after school each day are a hell of a lot worse than my book."

My excuses are running out. "I should stay home and work on my designs."

He looks at me patiently. "I spoke to Gabriel earlier and he said you were ahead of schedule."

There's absolutely no way I'm getting out of this. "If it's important to you, I'll do it, but I want you to know that I'm a hostile reader."

"You've been reading that manuscript I gave you, haven't you?"

I have. I wasn't going to. My plan all along was to give that flash drive back to Nicholas, but I decided to keep it. I know that it meant a lot to him that I asked for the book in the first place, so I made a vow that I'd work my way through the entire book. I'm almost done and it's even more impressive than I anticipated. It's no wonder Joe cashed in on it the way that he did. Nicholas writes with an intensity that's captivating. I got lost in his words more than once.

"I have read a lot of it," I confess. "I love it. I'm proud of you."

"You're proud of me?" He places both of his hands in the center of his chest. "I feel the very same way about you, Sophia. Your life will change when Ella Kara launches. My only hope is that you won't forget about me. Don't leave me in your dust."

"I'll never be as famous as you are."

He pulls back and looks me right in the eye. "When I'm with you, I just want to be Nicholas. I don't want to be famous."

"You are just Nicholas to me." My lips twitch. "I went to see Noah Foster a few weeks ago to get a new headshot and we talked about you."

"Noah's a good guy. He did my headshot a year or so ago."

My eyes wander to the photograph hanging on his wall of the beautiful, nude woman that Noah took. "He told me that I reminded him of his wife. I don't know her, but it felt like a huge compliment at the time."

"He doesn't hand out many."

Noah's words mean even more now. "He told me that it was good that I didn't care that you were Nicholas Wolf, but I do care. I care that you have such passion for your work that you captivate people all over the world. I care that you have taken years to hone your craft and that you're dedicated to telling the best story you possibly can."

His eyes soften. "Your opinion matters to me, Sophia. If you're proud of me, I'm capable of doing anything."

"Next week we'll go to that school and I already know I'll walk out at the end of the night in awe of you."

"I feel the same way whenever I talk to Gabriel about you."

"I'll go with you and I'll read to the kids if you want me to, but when we're done, you have to promise me one thing." I lean up to brush my lips over his.

"I'll do anything for you. You know that."

"Promise me that you'll let me teach you how to play that beautiful instrument behind us."

His fingers trace a path along my collarbone before dipping down to the buttons on the front of my dress. "I'll try and learn to play the piano if you'll promise me that you'll let me feast on you tonight."

"I promise," I say as I watch his hands open my dress and reach for the clasp at the front of my black bra.

***

"I'm going to be on Rise and Shine." I smile broadly. "Do you remember the first time you were on that show, Cadence? Now, I'm going on too."

"You're a star," Cadence singsongs with a huge grin on her face. "You know that old saying, Soph. If you can make it on Rise and Shine, you can make it anywhere."

"It's a song." I toss her a mock scowl. "If you can make it in this city, you can make it anywhere."

"That's exactly what you're doing." Her hand rubs her chin. "I'd say you officially made it already."

"That's why I made this lunch reservation." We near the entrance to Hibiscus. "I want to celebrate my upcoming appearance on the show that's already launched your career and will soon launch mine."

"You don't need a short appearance on a morning television show to launch your career." She scans the exterior of the building. "I keep telling you that as soon as Ella Kara launches, you'll be a household name."

"My clothing designers aren't household names." I point out as I reach for the handle of the door.

She steps in before I do. "You're launching a collection that is affordable, Soph. That means that you'll have millions of eyes on it. You're going to blow up the fashion world. Mark my words."

"Sophia Reese," I say to the woman at the hostess desk before I turn back to Cadence. "I hope you don't mind that we came here. I didn't eat much when we were here for the party. I want to try the smoked trout."

"I'm having one of everything." She looks over my shoulder into the busy dining room. "This place is hopping."

It is. Dining out with Cadence is an experience onto itself. Her eye is critical of everything and her palate professionally trained. She knows what works and doesn't work and it's not uncommon for her to ask to speak to the chef after we've been served our entrees. The majority of the time she does that to commend them on a job well done. If she does have critical feedback, she always presents it in a kind and respectful manner.

I follow her as the hostess takes us to our table. Cadence observes everything, soaking in the subtle details of the design and the table layout.

"Whoever is behind this restaurant is a genius," she says to the hostess once we're seated. "Is the manager available? My name is Chef Sutton."

It's rare for her to pull out the chef card. I like when she does. I want her to be proud of what she's accomplished in her short career.

The hostess beams as Cadence speaks to her. "I know exactly who you are. You're marrying Tyler Monroe."

"I am," Cadence grouses. She's proud of Tyler, but her accomplishments are often overshadowed by his.

"Are you thinking of shooting your segment here, Den?" I interject myself into the conversation. "I thought you were set on showcasing that new restaurant on the Upper East Side and not this one."

The hostess straightens, her hand reaching out to tentatively touch Den's shoulder. "You're here on official business, Chef? I had no idea. Your meal is on the house and I'll get the manager out as soon as possible."

With that, she takes off toward the kitchen.

"I'm not thinking of showcasing this place on my show." Cadence narrows her gaze at me. "I can deal with people thinking Tyler is a better chef than I am."

"I can't." I meet her gaze and hold it. "I want the entire world to know that my best friend is an incredible chef. If I have to tell every person I meet, I will."

"You're the best, Soph." She nibbles on one of the pieces of bread that were already on the table when we sat down. "I only wanted to talk to the manager so I could tell them I admire their style."

I open the menu in front of me and scan the offerings. "You'll do that and then we'll eat for free."

Chapter 28

Sophia

"I'm sorry I had to go to the washroom again." Cadence moves to take her seat back at our table. "I think the baby is sitting on my bladder today."

"Is it uncomfortable?" I eye her stomach. "You're getting a lot bigger now."

"He's growing." She smiles gently. "I'm getting anxious to meet him. I want him to understand how much we love him as soon as he's born."

He'll know. How could he not? Cadence is going to be an incredible mother. She'll nurture that baby with all the love she has to give, and Tyler will do the same. Firi Monroe won't want for a thing and by the time he's in nursery school, he'll have a more sophisticated palate than most adults have.

"I think I may shoot a segment here." Cadence raises her water glass in the air. "Your idea was brilliant. I need to start using the platform I have for good."

"Good in what sense?" I tap the edge of my water glass against hers in a subtle toast to her new idea.

"It's not easy opening a restaurant in this city. Most shut down within a year and those that do manage to claw their way to semi-success, aren't guaranteed a thing. One of Tyler's friends from culinary school was forced to close two of his restaurants this past year."

"That's shitty."

"If I can bring people through the door of a restaurant that's newly opened, that can help them establish a regular customer base right out of the gate."

Her kindness is shining through right now. I saw it when she was talking to the manager before we ate our lunch.

"I think it's a great idea, Den."

"I'm going to go back and find the manager." She pushes the chair back to stand again. "I think it might be worthwhile for her to offer a discount on a menu item the day the segment airs. I want to run that by her."

"Go." I wave my hand at her. "I'm going to finish my dessert before I head back to work."

She doesn't hesitate before she takes off back in the direction of the kitchen. She's a woman on a mission that I think will give new restaurateurs a chance they'd otherwise never receive.

"Can I get you anything else?" Our server appears next to me

I look at her briefly before my eyes settle on a table behind her. "I'm good."

Her gaze follows mine as she turns to look too. "That's exactly who you think is it. That's the one and only Nicholas Wolf. I love his work and the fact that he's so easy on the eyes doesn't hurt either."

She's right. It doesn't hurt. What does hurt is the fact that the man I love told me earlier that he was heading to Boston today to do a pre-release interview for *Action's Cause*. He didn't tell me that he was having lunch in New York with Lilly Parker and a beautiful black-haired woman who right now is holding tightly to his hand.

***

"Nicholas," I say his name softly as I approach his table. "I thought you were headed to Boston today."

"Sophia?" He's on his feet instantly, obviously unsettled by my sudden appearance by his side. "What are you doing here?"

Catching you with your hand where it shouldn't be?

"Having lunch," I say calmly. I want to add that it should be obvious to him that I'm at Hibiscus because they serve food and I work a few blocks away. "What are you doing here?"

"I mentioned that I'd be meeting Lilly for lunch one day. It turns out today was the day."

But you said you wanted me to be there.

I shake off the all-consuming feelings of self-pity. That explains why he's here with Lilly, but the dark-haired woman who looks like she's salivating at the sight of his ass is still a mystery to me. "It's nice to see you again, Lilly."

"It's always good to see you, Sophia. I hear that you're heading your own collection now. You've come a long way since we worked together."

I have, and I'm proud of every single step I've taken since I first moved to New York. I turn my attention to the mystery woman and extend my hand to her. "I'm Sophia Reese."

"Del Burnette." Her hand lands in mine with no recognition of who I am in relation to Nicholas.

"Are you a friend of Lilly's?"

She shakes her head as a high pitched giggle bubbles from her throat. "I'm an old friend of Nick's."

By friend she means lover. I see it her body language. She had him, and now, she wants him again.

"I need to get back to work." I do. It's not a lie. I'm not going to let Nicholas or his lunch dates throw me off course. I have to present the final one of my design ideas to Sasha this afternoon. I have some last minute details to get in place before I do.

"I'll walk you out."

I turn at the sound of his voice. "I can find my own way out, Nicholas."

"I insist." His hand drops to my lower back.

I don't argue. I won't question him here. I can't. If I start in on that, I'll lose focus on what's important to me right now. That's my work. It's what I'll have when this falls apart, so I have to keep it together.

"Lilly called me last minute to ask if I'd meet her here." He speaks as we walk. "Del saw me across the room and sat down to catch up."

"You've slept with her?"

He stops us both as we near the entrance. "Yes, Sophia. It was a long time ago."

"She'd like it to happen again now."

"She would, but it won't."

I edge closer to the door, aware that I'm already late getting back to work. "You were holding her hand, Nicholas."

"I was."

"Can you explain why?"

He moves to allow a couple to brush past on their way out. "This isn't a conversation I want to have when you're in a rush."

"Is the answer that complicated?" I ask. "All I want to know is why you were holding hands."

"I'll explain, Sophia but I can see that you're in a hurry to get back to work."

I'm frustrated and I know that's apparent in my expression. My face is heating, my back tensing into countless tight knots. "You're making this more complicated than it needs to be. Just answer the question."

"It's not a cut and dry answer, Sophia." His tone lowers. "It's complex and I need time to explain my relationship with Del to you."

Relationship? The word hits me with the force of a slap in the face.

"When can you explain it?" I'm impatient and I don't give a fuck if he knows it or not. "You can come to see me at work when you're done here."

"I can't." He reaches for my hand but I pull back. "Sophia, please understand. There's nothing for you to worry about."

"Come to my office when you're done here and we'll talk," I repeat. "I want to talk about this today."

"I won't have time." He glances back over his shoulder. "I'm taking a late afternoon flight out to Boston. I'll be spending the night there."

"Why? I thought it was one interview. You said you'd be gone half a day at most."

"Cheyenne scheduled another tomorrow morning. Flying back and forth won't work. I'll stay the night and be back here tomorrow afternoon. I'll call you tonight and we can talk."

"No." I shake off the urge I have inside to stomp my feet and scream at him. "I don't want to talk on the phone. You said this is complex, so I want it to be in person. I'll meet you tomorrow night at your place."

"I love you, Sophia. I need you to understand that is a fact that will never change."

Words are words. Actions speak for themselves.

"Have a safe flight, Nicholas." I hold onto my words I know he wants to hear because his actions are making me question everything. "I'll see you tomorrow."

Chapter 29

Nicholas

Telling Sophia that I almost married the woman she saw me holding hands with, wasn't something I could do in the crowded entrance of a restaurant when I knew I had to board a plane hours later.

Del may be part of my past, but she inches into my life at regular intervals. Unlike Franco, she hasn't crossed over into stalker yet. Del is more discreet, her approach subtle.

We met when I was in therapy after Briella's death. Del was on her way out of the office when I was on my way in. That happened twice before we fucked in a stairwell without any formal introductions. It was intense and marred by the pain we were both in. I'd lost the woman I loved and Del had lost a father she hated.

At the time, I didn't realize that I viewed her as a second chance. I could protect her from her demons and give her pleasure all while avoiding falling in love with her. I felt nothing for her beyond pity and lust. She proposed to me on a rooftop one night and I accepted. I was drunk on cheap beer and the idea of a second chance at something that would fill the pit of desperation I was feeling.

Once I sobered up, I ended it.

For years after we broke up, she'd call me at regular intervals. I'd take those calls at face value. I knew that she was only calling to see if I was interested in hooking up. I was back then. I'd meet her for dinner, we'd go back to her place and by the time I'd left, we would have screwed, laughed about the good old days and then said our goodbyes again.

She was like a habit I couldn't break until I had to. She fell into the pit of addiction and as her need for her next fix grew, my concern for her did as well.

I stepped back because partying with her suddenly included her being high and wanting to take risks that almost ruined me.

One night we went to a member's only club in mid-town and as we fucked in a room filled with nude bodies and the sounds and the smells of sex, I saw my face in a wall of mirrors that was designed to heighten the pleasure of everyone in the room.

My reflection showed a man lost in a crowd of thrill-seeking addicts. It also showed a tanned woman being fucked from behind by a man. That woman had been to every book signing I'd ever held and when our eyes met in the mirror's reflection, she offered her brow in an invitation to fuck her if I wanted. I fled.

I ended things with Del but helped her navigate through her recovery. She needed me by her side and I needed to know she'd be all right.

"I asked if you were good with the new tour schedule." Cheyenne walks through the doorway of our adjoining rooms. "I need your go-ahead before I confirm these dates."

I read them over. It's a schedule I would have approved without a second thought six months ago, but that was pre-Sophia. I don't want to be away from her, but I know my career's success is based solely on my fan base. I need to see them and interact with them if I expect to keep selling books.

"I want to run it by Sophia." I don't bother to look at my publicist. I know what I'll see on her face. Disappointment.

"Get on that today or tomorrow, Nick." She picks up the room service menu. "Are you eating here tonight or do you want to hit the town?"

I've been checking flights back to Manhattan but it makes no sense. I tried calling Sophia but it went straight to voicemail. I know she was pissed that I didn't explain things with Del to her earlier at the restaurant but I need time to reassure her that there's nothing left between me and any woman from my past. I hadn't thought of Del in months before today.

"There's an Axel here. Can you get us a table, Cheyenne?"

"I've never been to Axel Boston. Axel New York is a personal favorite of mine."

I know that. She reminds me almost weekly. Cheyenne has expensive taste in food, fashion, and men. I can only satisfy the first, so I do on occasion.

"I'll drop your name." Her fingers skim over her phone's screen. "If they know Nicholas Wolf is in town and ready to enjoy a meal at their restaurant, they'll give us the best table in the place."

"Make it happen." I get up from the uncomfortable couch I've been sitting on. "I'll shower and be ready in an hour."

***

"I'm leaving, Cheyenne." I toss my napkin onto the half-eaten plate of food in front of me. "I'm going back to New York now."

"Now?" She takes a sip of the way-too-expensive wine she ordered with the pricey appetizer and entree. "You can't go. I doubt you'll make it back in time for your interview in the morning."

"Cancel it." I pocket my phone. "That call I left the table to take is about something urgent. It's personal so don't bother asking. It's none of your business."

"And he slides right back into asshole mode." She smiles. "Are you folks all right? Is this about your brothers?"

"They're fine." I button my suit jacket. "It's not about any of them. I have to go back to Manhattan to meet someone. This is more important than the interview so reschedule."

"They might not agree to that." There's a subtle warning in her tone. "If you keep canceling shit like this, it's going to impact you in the long run."

"You'll smooth it over. I pay you to do that."

"It's Sophia, isn't it?" Her brow quirks. "Did you have a lover's quarrel and now you have to rush back to the city so you can kiss and make up?"

She can't possibly know how much I wish that were it. "Mind your own business, Cheyenne and don't drink me into poverty. I'll put a limit on that credit card I gave you if you spend too much tonight."

"You'd never do that to me." She leans forward. "I'm a call away if you need anything, Nick. I hope you know that."

"I do." I'm tempted to embrace her but I don't. "I'll talk to you tomorrow so don't inundate me with calls and texts. Handle this on your own."

"You've got it boss and say *hi* to Sophia for me."

I will if I find her.

Chapter 30

Nicholas

"Tell me how the fuck this happened?" I grab the front of Crew's coat. "I want to know who messed up."

He's calm. I see it immediately in his eyes. "I can't tell you how but I'll tell you what I know, Nick. I need you to sit and take a breath. You're not doing Sophia any favors by losing it."

I sit in a chair across from him. We're in his office. It's after two a.m. It took me three hours to get a seat on a flight back to New York.

During the time I sat in the terminal waiting to board my concern for Sophia went from mild to intense. At first, I thought she was ignoring my calls and texts because she was pissed that I didn't take the time to explain my connection with Del to her. When Crew called me to say that her phone had been found in an alley outside of Foster Enterprises, my world instantly went dark.

"He's not in Florida." Crew picks up printed copy of Franco Abano's mug shot. "He didn't fly out. There's no record of him on a bus or train. The best we can figure is that he rented a car and drove here."

"He's here?" I stand again. "That fucker is in New York?"

"I called Gabriel Foster an hour ago. He had his security team pull footage from the cameras outside the Foster Enterprises building. Franco was there. He kept his distance, but he was outside mid-afternoon."

"He has her." My voice cracks. "That prick took her. Someone must have seen it."

"The police are on it, Nick. I called Sebastian while you were in the air. He contacted someone in missing persons, and I just got off the phone with them. They'll be at Foster bright and early to review that security footage and to interview anyone who went in or out of the building around the time Sophia left."

"Where would he take her?" I pinch the bridge of my nose trying to think. "He must have rented a room. Are you checking that out?"

"As we speak. We have someone at her place too. If he tries to take her back there, we'll be on him immediately. I need you to remember something, Nick. Listen to me."

I look across the desk at where he's standing in front of the windows of his office. "What?"

"He's in love with her." He exhales harshly. "He doesn't want to hurt her. He won't hurt her. I believe that. I need you to believe that too."

"She's scared as fuck right now." I clench my fists at my side. "You know that she is."

"I know she's strong. Sophia is the most resourceful woman I know." He cups his jaw in his hand. "If anyone can talk their way out of this, it's her."

"What if there's no way out?"

"I refuse to believe that." He points at his phone. "I called Cadence. She's going to fill Sophia's folks in. I've arranged a private jet to bring them here."

It's all shit I should have handled myself but I'm damn grateful he's done it.

"I hurt her before I left New York today." I look him straight in the eye. "She saw me with Del and wanted an explanation."

"That would have taken all day."

I filled Crew in on the details of what happened between Del and me one night over a case of beer. He understood and told me back then to steer clear of her. I should have refused when she asked to sit next to me today. I should never have let her touch me.

"I had all day. I could have given her that."

"You'll give her that when you see her again." He moves closer. "We'll find her, Nick and when we do, you can make things right."

I hope I get that fucking chance. If I don't, I know my heart won't survive this loss.

***

"Sophia tells us that you're an author." Her mother dabs a tissue over her cheeks. "We haven't read your book yet, but it's on our list."

I smile weakly at her. Doris and Robert Reese are good people. They're strong. I sensed it when we met in the lobby of Foster Enterprises. Her mom embraced me and her dad offered his hand. His grip was weakened by the sorrow on his face.

He feels he let his little girl down. I'm the one who did. I didn't press Sophia about the security detail I wanted on her. I let it slide because I thought I had time. That piece of shit Franco was in Florida, dating another woman. I had no idea he'd bail on that and head to New York to take Sophia away from us all.

"Can I get you anything?" Cadence approaches us from the left. She's been here all day with her husband. She's spent most of the time crying in his arms.

"Not a thing, dear." Doris leans her head against Cadence's arm. "I think you should go home and rest. This stress can't be good for the baby."

"He's strong." Her voice cracks. "He's like Sophia."

Doris sniffles her way through a response. "Sophia won't let him hurt her. She'll fight back. I taught my daughter to fight."

"We taught her well." Robert kisses his wife's cheek. "I'm going to find the detective we met earlier. I'll see if she has an update."

I nod as he walks toward the door of the conference room that Gabriel arranged for us to use as a meeting place. He's been in and out himself all day; his brow etched with worry.

"Do you think there will be some leads from the press conference we had?" Doris turns to face me directly. "I think Franco will give her back to us when he sees how much we love her."

Franco is a sick bastard who doesn't give a shit about anyone else. The press conference that was held an hour ago was meant to draw tips from anyone who had seen Sophia or Franco in the past twenty-four hours. His picture, along with hers, splashed across the screen before Sophia's parents took the podium. They both cried through an emotional explanation of what she meant to them.

I couldn't keep it together. With Crew by my side, I sobbed as I watched as the city learned that a beautiful, talented and loving woman was missing and a cold-hearted stalker was the man responsible.

"I think the press conference might change everything." I rest my hands on her shoulders. "Your daughter will come back. I need her to. I love her too much to lose her."

"She loves you too, dear." She reaches up to cup my cheek. "You're the first boy our Sophia has ever loved."

Chapter 31

Sophia

I watch as Franco pours a can of something red into a pot on the stove. We're in the basement of a brownstone in Lower Manhattan. He brought me here yesterday. I came willingly.

I decided to take a shortcut to the subway after work. It was just starting to rain, and the dress I'm wearing is too special to risk the long walk around the corner. Darting through the alley meant time saved and fewer stains on the fabric of the skirt. As soon as I saw Franco step in front of me with a small knife in one hand, I froze.

I didn't scream. I didn't try and run. Instead, I walked with him to a rusted car he pointed at that was parked less than ten feet away.

I got in the back seat when he told me to and then I watched in silence as he opened the other back passenger door so he could help the young boy who had been holding his hand, get in.

"Elroy," I whisper to that same boy who is now resting his head on my lap. "Are you hungry?"

He nods.

I spent all of last night wide awake watching Franco interact with the child. At first, I had no idea who he was but as the evening wore on, Elroy spoke. His mother and Franco were friends at one time. Elroy lived on the streets and Franco would stop and offer whatever he could to them both. When Elroy's mother was taken to the hospital yesterday, Franco stood by and watched before he took the child by the hand and led him away from the uncertainty of life in the same foster care system Franco himself had grown up in.

"It's almost ready," Franco calls back over his shoulder. "I only have enough for you two."

I have no appetite other than a hunger for contact with someone I know. I didn't realize that I'd dropped my phone until we got here. I searched for it in the pockets of my coat but it wasn't there.

"Elroy feels warm." I rest my lips against the forehead of the five-year-old again. "I think he needs to see a doctor, Franco."

"Our son is fine." Franco turns to look at us both. "I knew you'd be a good mom, Sophia. Our son is going to grow up and tell people that you're the best of the best."

He's delusional. When I first heard him tell Elroy to call him dad, I saw the look of confusion on the brown haired boy's face. He's as terrified as I am which means I can't leave his side.

"I think you can give a child ibuprofen when they're fevered," I ignore Franco's ramblings about our make believe family. "Can't you go get some, Franco?"

"And waste time being with my wife and son?" he scoffs. "No way. This soup will help. He'll fall asleep and be fine by morning."

He won't be. His skin is clammy and his eyes barren. I know a lot of that has to do with what he witnessed back on that street in Florida when his mother was taken away. He has to be terrified now, wondering if she's survived and whether he'll ever see her again.

"Let me go get it." I reach out my hand toward him. "Please, baby. He needs help."

The pet name does the trick. The grin on Franco's face is genuine and broad. "People might be looking for you, beautiful. I don't want anyone to take you away from me."

He's right. People will be looking for me. It's been almost a full day now since I got in his car. Nicholas will be frantic by now. My parents will be too.

I go to Plan B. "On the ride here I noticed there's a pharmacy a block from here. We can order the medicine and they'll bring it right to us."

"They'll bring it here? They'll come to our place?"

"A delivery boy will." I try and laugh. "Most of them are teenagers. The last one I had didn't even look up from his phone when I gave him the money for my order."

He contemplates what I'm saying. "You really think our son needs that to get better?"

It shouldn't be this easy. I'm drawing him in hook, line, and sinker. He loves this child. That's obvious and if I have to play on that to get this little boy back to his mother, I will. "Fevers can get dangerous quickly, babe. If we stop it now, he'll feel better in a day or two and maybe then we can take him to the park and for ice cream."

"How do I do this?" He tugs his phone from the pocket of his pants. His long dark hair shields his face as he stares at the screen. "Do I just call?"

"I usually do my orders online." I hold out my palm. "I can order that way. It would be the fastest."

He eyes me before his gaze drops to Elroy. "That won't work. I'll call and see if they can bring it. I have a credit card I can use."

I know there's no way in hell that credit card bears his real name. "Is the card stolen?"

He nods. "It probably won't work by now."

"We can pay cash." I scramble for my purse. "You call and I'll see how much money I have on me. Tell them we need children's ibuprofen and get some candy too."

"You think of everything." He turns his back and pours the soup into two ceramic mugs. "I'll call while you two eat. We'll have our boy feeling better in no time flat."

Chapter 32

Nicholas

"You're sure?" I look down at the police detective assigned to the case. I never caught her name. I wasn't paying enough attention to care. I can't form a logical thought at this point.

"It's from her." She stands in front of me, her hands cradling her phone. "A hostage negotiation team is there and they've established communication with Abano. Before you ask, you're not going. No one but our members will be allowed within a two-block radius."

"Can I see it at least?" I glance at her phone. "You must have a copy of it. I can verify her handwriting."

"There's no need." She shakes her head. "It's a vital piece of evidence, Mr. Wolf. I can't show it to you."

"Tell me what it said," I press. "That fucking television in the conference room is on. I heard the breaking news. I know it was a dollar bill. She wrote on it."

"Dammit." She shakes her head. "News leaks from our department faster than we can keep on top of it."

"What did it say?"

"She's safe."

"What else?" I'm not an idiot. I saw the change in the detective's demeanor. She left an hour ago after getting a call on her cell. She's back now and jumpy as shit.

"You need to take a seat, Mr. Wolf, and wait for another update."

"I need you to tell me why the fuck it is taking forever for you to get her out of that building."

"There are protocols in place in this type of situation."

"According to the goddamn news, the police have been on the scene for more than an hour. Give me two minutes with that fucker Abano and I'll buy Sophia's freedom."

She leans forward. "This is off the record and a favor to your brother, Sebastian, so keep this between you and me."

"Spit it out," I growl. "If Sophia's still in danger, I want in there. I know I can reason with the man. Money can buy anything. Abano has a price and I'll pay it."

"He's willing to let her go, but she won't leave."

"That's fucking bullshit." I step back. "You're a fucking liar."

"Watch it." Her hand rises in the air between us.

"If he gave her the chance to walk out of there alive, she would."

"She won't because there's a child in there with them. Abano kidnapped a five-year-old in Florida. That little boy is the reason Sophia won't come out."

***

I rest my head in my hands. It shouldn't surprise me that she's willing to risk her own life to save a child she doesn't know. I wouldn't expect less of her, yet I want her out. I want her safe and back in my arms.

"She's going to come out of this, Nick." Robert takes a seat next to me. "She's on the cusp of good things. Fate won't steal that from her. She's too much good in her life."

"Tell me about her." I try to level my tone. Her parents know nothing about the child that's trapped in there with Sophia. I don't want to add to their burden by telling them that she stayed behind to protect him. "I want to know more about her."

"You already know that she plays the piano." He raps his fingertips against his knee. "She's damn good."

"The best I've ever heard, sir."

"Bob." His gaze drops. "You'll call me Bob."

I will. I hope for many years to come. "I have a piano at my place. She plays for me sometimes."

"I'm envious." He chuckles. "I miss hearing her play. Maybe while we're here, we can stop by and she'll give us a private concert."

"She'd love that." I believe she would. She's only told me limited details about her relationship with her folks. I didn't press because I saw no need to.

"I know that she loves you." Something passes briefly over his expression, but it's gone before I can read it. "I always hoped my little girl would find a man who loved her as much as I do. You're proving today that you do."

My eyes well with tears. God isn't going to give me this moment to steal it away from me in my next breath. Sophia needs to come out of this so I can ask this man for her hand in marriage one day. I want to be part of this family. I want Sophia to be part of mine. I haven't called my folks down here yet. I've talked to my mom twice, both times she told me she'd light a candle and pray for Sophia. She told me she loves her already since I do.

"I love her," I say in a sob. "I'll never stop."

He moves to embrace me. His frail hands patting my back as he tells me over and over that everything is going to be fine. I believe him. My Sophia is coming back to me. She has to.

Chapter 33

Sophia

"Please, please be careful with him," I say to the EMT who is cradling Elroy in his arms. "He has a fever and he's weak."

He nods as he heads for the open door of the ambulance. It's almost dark outside, but I can clearly make out the number of police cars, ambulances and fire trucks that have gathered on this quiet street.

My plan was risky, but it worked. When the delivery boy buzzed to be let in, I handed Franco the money. He looked it over before he exchanged it for the children's ibuprofen. The guy who made the delivery counted it and then complained that it was a dollar short. I reached into my purse, pulled out the dollar I'd written on while Franco was on the phone placing the order and I ran it to the door and tucked it directly into the delivery guy's palm.

Then I prayed. I prayed that he would see the note I'd written on the back. It was as detailed as I could manage in the few moments I had to write it.

I knew that there was a good chance that the bill would be passed on to someone else before the ink was noticed, so I wrote my name, the date, the address of the building that I'd memorized when we first walked in and Elroy's first name and age. I was able to scribble the words *he's been kidnapped from Florida* before Franco ended the call.

"You need to go to the hospital, Sophia."

I turn toward the voice of a male detective. He was one of the first faces I saw when I carried Elroy from the building. He ran to me and scooped the crying boy from my arms. I was grateful, collapsing on the ground at his feet in tears before another man hauled me up and took me to safety. It was all a blur. All I knew at that moment was that we were safe and police officers were on their way into the building to arrest Franco.

"I should call someone." I look around the street. "I need to call my boyfriend. My parents must be worried sick."

"They're all waiting for you at the hospital." He motions toward the ambulance. "I'll ride with you and take your preliminary statement."

I look down at my shaking hands. "I want to thank whoever was talking to Franco on the phone. They got him to agree to let us go."

"When things settle down, I'll introduce you myself." He wraps his arms around my shoulder. "We can worry about that another day. Right now, we need to get you checked out."

"I'm fine." I wobble on my heels. "I'm worried about Elroy. I followed the directions on the bottle of ibuprofen. I gave him exactly what it said, but he was still so warm."

"You took great care of him, Sophia."

My hands shake. "He was confused. I tried to keep him quiet and calm."

"You did everything right."

"I didn't want him to hurt Elroy." I swallow hard. "I wanted him to see his mom again."

"He will." He helps me get into the back of the ambulance. "Once he's checked over, he'll be released to an aunt who flew in from Phoenix. She'll take care of him until his mom is back on her feet."

"I was scared." Tears stream down my face. "I was scared I'd never see the people I love again."

"We're on our way to see them now." He takes a seat next to a female EMT. "It's over, Sophia. You're free."

***

There are so many faces it's hard to register who they all are. I hear my mom's voice and then my dad's. Cadence is crying and Crew is somewhere telling someone to get the fuck out of his way. I smile under the oxygen mask as I'm wheeled through the entrance of the ER.

Nicholas is close. I can sense him before I see him.

"Sophia?" His voice is like a beacon to me. I raise my head, trying desperately to find him. I do. He's to my left, pushing past Dexie to get to me.

"Sophia." He stops the movement of the stretcher with his hands, stilling the two EMTs in place. "Did he hurt you?"

I shake my head to the side.

"She's good." The detective says from somewhere nearby. "Abano is in custody. Sophia is fine. The child is fine because of her."

"Child?" My mother looks down at me. "Are you pregnant, Sophia?"

I hear a chorus of laughs surround me. The sound is a symphony to me. It's pure happiness. Joy radiates from the people I love.

"I have no information on that." The detective waves his hands in the air with a chuckle. "There was a boy with Abano. Sophia stayed with him. She protected him and brought him out alive."

"Sophia," my mom whispers my name as she kisses my cheek. "You're an angel. You are an angel sent from heaven."

"That she is." Nicholas reaches for my hand. "She's my angel."

Chapter 34

Sophia

"Did my mom put you up to this?" I stare up at the doctor. He's older than me by a few years; the hair on his temples is giving way to gray from brown.

"Your mom?" he questions back. "I don't follow."

"You're good." I rest my head on the pillow. "She made a joke about me being pregnant when I was brought in. I know she's persuasive. You did a good job though. I almost believed you."

His mouth cuts into a wide grin. "Denial is a very common reaction to an unplanned pregnancy, Sophia."

"You can drop the act." I rub my belly. "There isn't a baby in here. I use the pill and my boyfriend always wraps it up tight."

"Neither of those is foolproof." He skims his fingers over a tablet in his hands. "I'll show you what is foolproof; the results of your bloodwork."

He turns the tablet toward me. I try to focus on the medical terms and the corresponding numbers next to them. "This is how you'd feel if I handed you the pattern for a dress."

He chuckles. "You're in surprisingly good spirits for someone who went through an ordeal like that."

"I'm alive." I sigh deeply. "I also think I'm in shock. It feels like a dream; almost like I was watching it all from the sidelines."

"I'm going to send someone down to talk to you." He moves closer to the bed. "She's skilled in dealing with situations like this."

"I have someone to talk to." I rub my fingers across my lips. "His name is Liam Wolf. He was in to see me earlier today. We talked about what happened yesterday. I'll talk to him more."

"Liam is one of the best." He turns the tablet back around. "He's a good guy and I think he'll be an amazing uncle."

"I'm not pregnant." I feel a stir in my heart. "I would know if I was."

"You are pregnant." He leans his hand on the bed. "You're not more than a few weeks along. It's early and anything can happen, but today, at this minute, you're pregnant."

***

"You didn't go home, did you?" I look at the clothes he's wearing. "You were dressed in that when I was first brought in."

"I've been sitting on a chair outside your door." Nicholas tilts his chin toward the door of my private room. "The doctor said you needed to sleep, so I camped out there. They tried to kick me out, but I pulled the *'I'm Nicholas Wolf'* card out of my back pocket."

I stare up at his face. He's so beautiful. He's going to be an incredible dad. "Did that work?"

"Not at all." He half-smiles. "Apparently, the people who work here are too busy to read."

I pat the bed. "Sit. I want to talk about something."

He pulls on the thighs of his jeans before he sits next to me. He reaches for my hand. "We can talk about Franco. I want you to feel strong. I'm here to listen to you."

I can't imagine what he went through when I was missing. As much fear as I had, I knew that Franco wouldn't hurt me. He loved me. It was in a sick, demented way but it was the shield that kept me and Elroy safe.

"No." My hand goes to my throat. I feel my airway constrict when I think about the small apartment that Franco took us to. "I don't want to talk about him right now."

"If it's about Del, I'm sorry, Sophia. I wanted to explain it at Hibiscus, but I'm committed to being completely honest with you. The shit with Del is over. I need you to at least know that right now. There's more to the story, and it will take time to tell but that story is over. It has been for a long time."

"It's not about her." I appreciate the offering. I haven't given Del a lot of thought since Franco appeared in that alleyway. All of my thoughts about Nicholas the past few days have been about the moments we've spent together.

I imagined being back at his apartment. I closed my eyes while Elroy slept and thought about the things Nicholas has said to me. He loves me. I know that he does. Whatever took place between him and Del is in the past.

"Did I seem jealous at Hibiscus?" I squeeze his hand.

"Maybe a little." He holds his index finger and thumb an inch apart. "I don't mind the jealousy."

"You don't?"

"It's part of you. I love every part of you, Sophia."

The weight of the past few days suddenly hits me like a freight train. I can't stop my emotions. They flow out of me quickly, violently. I sob while I cling to him. "I thought about you every single second I was gone. I kept thinking about how you would feel if I didn't come back."

"That was never an option." His voice is heavy with emotion. "I knew you'd be back. I felt it inside."

"I understand more now." I pull back to look into his tear-stained face. "You've been through so much."

"Me?" He taps his chest. "You're the one who saved a child's life, Sophia. You're the one who was held hostage by a lunatic."

"You're the one who saw the person you love after she'd just taken her last breath."

"Sophia," he whispers my name as he pulls me close to him. His lips press against my forehead. "I love you."

"I didn't know what to do." I shake in his arms, my breathing increasing. "Franco told me I could go but I refused. I couldn't leave Elroy in there. I'll never forget the look of terror on that little boy's face when I first saw him standing in the alley with Franco."

He exhales sharply. "That memory will fade. Weeks, months and then years will pass and you'll start to forget the details. It won't be as vivid and one day you'll have such a full life that the memory of yesterday won't be sharp or clear anymore."

"Do you promise?"

"I'll help you heal from this, Sophia. Let me do that for you."

Chapter 35

Nicholas

I watch her pick at the lunch that a hospital orderly brought for her. If I had known the food smelled and tasted like this, I would have sent Liam back to my place to make her a grilled cheese sandwich.

I was grateful when he showed up at the hospital. He'd been dealing with a work-related crisis for most of the night, but once he had a break, he was here. I introduced him to Sophia and then left them alone. I didn't ask what they discussed, but when he left her room, he told me she was strong. He likes her and once she's feeling up to it, she'll talk to him again.

"I think they'll discharge me this afternoon. I'm not dehydrated anymore." She pushes the tray toward me. "Can we stop on our way home to get a burger and some chili fries?"

I furrow my brow. "I can run out and get that for you now. I wouldn't be gone more than twenty minutes."

She nods. "Can you get some of those chocolate candies that you keep in that dish on your kitchen counter?"

"The one I have to keep refilling after you eat them all?"

Her face brightens. "Those are the ones. I think they would taste delicious on the fries."

I scowl. "You're going to put candy on the chili fries?"

"I can't decide if that would taste better or maybe strawberry yogurt."

I sit on the bed next to her again. "All of this shit you're talking about sounds disgusting."

"You better get used to it." She lowers her shoulders. "This is just the beginning, Nicholas."

"The beginning of what?"

"Crazy pregnancy cravings." Her eyes drop to the front of the hospital gown she's wearing.

My insides collapse. My heart bursts. "Sophia."

"The doctor told me earlier." She shakes away a flood of tears. "I don't know how, Nicholas. I mean I know how. You probably broke through the condom because sometimes you lose control."

"You're having a baby?" I place my hand on her stomach. "My baby?"

"I'm going to ignore that last question." She covers my hand with hers. "We're having a baby, but the doctor said it's very early and anything can happen."

I know that. My mother had four beautiful children but wanted more. I watched her suffer through three miscarriages before she finally gave into the idea that her family was complete.

"I don't want to tell anyone else yet," she continues. "We'll wait until we're sure that everything is good and then we can have a party."

"A party?"

"A celebration of the baby's life and my life. Your life. Our life." She nods slowly. "Cadence is going to scream when I tell her, but I'll wait. I want to wait."

"Do you think you'll have enough willpower to wait?"

I watch her stare at our hands. Her gaze trained to her stomach. "If we are supposed to have this baby, it will happen. If it doesn't, it means it's not our turn yet. I want to wait. I don't want to break my mom's heart if I don't have to."

"We'll wait."

"Are you happy, Nicholas?" she asks, even though she already knows the answer to that question.

"I've never been happier."

***

"I want you to move in with me, Sophia." I look around the living room of her apartment. "Does all of this furniture belong to you?"

"No." She shakes her head faintly. "Everything but my sewing machine and my clothing belongs to Cadence."

"It'll be an easy move. We can pack up your things now."

She pats the couch next to where she's sitting. "Sit with me. We need to talk about this."

"Talk about what?" I cross my legs and drape my arm around her shoulders.

She's been busy working on a new design since I brought her here from the hospital. I asked the Uber driver to stop so I could buy us each a burger and fries. Sophia laughed when I asked him to stop again at a candy store. She slapped my arm and told me she was kidding about the cravings. They'll come one day if this is all meant to be.

"I can't move in with you right now." She leans her head back against the cushion of the couch. "I have too much going on. The Ella Kara Collection is going to launch soon and this is where I do my best work. I can't change my life at a moment's notice."

"You better get used to doing just that." I tug on the corner of her sketchpad. "You're going to be a mom. A baby changes everything whenever the hell it wants to."

"The doctor said I was only a few weeks along." She pulls the sketchpad back into her lap. "That means I have months to get everything organized."

"You can organize from my place," I point out. "I'll rearrange some furniture and I'll make room in my office for your sewing machine."

"That leaves zero room for a nursery." She forms a circle with her fingers. "We can't have a baby there."

"I'll buy a new place."

"Not yet." Her voice is laced with exasperation. "We just found out a few hours ago that we're going to be parents. We don't need to rush into anything."

"I want to rush. I want to live with you. I want us to get married. I want our baby to have a beautiful life."

Her eyes wash with tears. "Don't ask me to marry you today. I can't hear that. Don't do it like that."

"Why not?" I get to my feet so I can stand in front of her. "I'll drop to my knee right here and now. Marry me, Sophia. Be my wife so we can be a family."

"No." She rises to her feet. "I won't marry you."

"What?" I push my hands in the front pockets of my jeans, my fingers skimming over the cold metal of my grandfather's ring. "Tell me why you won't."

Her eyes follow the path of my hands. "You're touching the ring you were going to give to Briella. You asked her to marry you the day you found out she was pregnant."

I stop and stare at her. "This is different, Sophia. This is us."

"I know you love me." She perches on her bare tiptoes to kiss my jaw. "Let me have my own story. Let my experience be my own."

"This is your experience." I embrace her tightly. "This is our experience."

"I'm not going anywhere. I want to stay here while I finish preparing for the launch of the line. I want you to work on your book and before this baby is born, everything will fall into place the way it's supposed to."

Chapter 36

Sophia

"These are all the stores that we're partnering with?" My gaze volleys between Gabriel and Sasha. "Is this for real?"

They laugh in unison.

"It's for real, Sophia." Sasha moves to stand next to me. "Early interest in the line is high. The pictures of the pieces that were leaked online went viral. Our sales department was inundated with calls from the get-go."

Leaked is a subjective term for what happened. Gabriel and I were at Axel NY sharing lunch when I threw an idea out at him. He was skeptical at first. He's old school which means you keep everything tightly under wraps until press day. I wanted to do something out of the box, and when I finally got him to agree to it, I took pictures of two of my most favorite pieces and uploaded them to a brand new Instagram account with every fashion related hashtag imaginable.

I tagged the stores I know are a good fit for the Ella Kara Collection and then I started following as many fashion bloggers as I could find. It only took three days before the post had more than ten thousand likes and by a week later that had grown to more than one hundred thousand. It didn't hurt that Claudia Stefano was one of the first to repost the picture with a caption that she wished she could showcase the collection in her boutiques. I remind myself to send her a bouquet of flowers to thank her for fulfilling my request.

"I'm stunned." I stare at the screen of Sasha's tablet. "We're still showing the line at Fashion Week?"

"We'll incorporate it into the Arilia show," Gabriel pipes up. "You'll present it and we want your full input on the models, accessories, everything related to the show."

"I can't wait for that." I push the tablet back to Sasha. "You'll come to the show, right?"

She decided last week that she'd start the long and winding trail to retirement. She's already cut down to two days a week and by the time Fashion Week is in full swing, she'll be making an appearance here once a month or less.

"I wouldn't miss it for the world."

I won't either. I'll be showing by then and everyone here will know that I'm having a baby. I'm not that far along now and although I can't see a difference in my body yet, I can feel it.

Our baby is still a secret that Nicholas and I cherish.

"Nick said you two could do dinner on Thursday, "Gabriel says smoothly. "It'll be good for the four of us to catch up."

It will be. Everyone has been treating me with kid gloves since the ordeal with Franco. I haven't talked a lot about what happened, but I have kept in close touch with Elroy's family. He's doing well, thriving and enjoying life in Arizona with his aunt and his mom.

Franco didn't bother to fight the charges brought against him. He has a court date approaching. He'll plead guilty which will mean he'll spend the rest of his life in prison.

"You feel up to having dinner, don't you, Sophia?"

I look at Sasha. It's not surprising that she'd be the one to ask me. She's kept watch over me since I came back to work. We didn't discuss what happened, but she hugged me tightly that first day. I've watched her navigate the press effortlessly when they've called in search of an interview and she even loaned me her company-supplied car and driver so I could sneak out each day to avoid the reporters who hung out in the lobby for more than a week.

Things have calmed. Life has returned to normal except for the issue that I have to discuss with Nicholas tonight.

"I would love to have dinner." I turn to Gabriel. "There's an open invitation for Sasha to join us, isn't there?"

"I've asked Sasha to have dinner with Isla and me for years, but," he's interrupted by a chime from his phone. He drops his gaze to it. "I need to go. Sasha knows she's always welcome at my home for dinner."

"I'll never show up." Sasha gives a curt nod to us both. "I like our relationship the way it is. Breaking bread together will change it."

"Once you're fully retired then?" Gabriel's eyes dance with humor. "That excuse will cease to exist once you're off the payroll."

"Good point. I suppose once I'm a free woman I'll have a change of heart."

I know she will. I see the affection between her and Gabriel. Even when she walks out of this design studio for the last time, Sasha will always be part of the Foster family.

***

"Who knew that your body would be even more beautiful when you're pregnant?" Nicholas runs his hands over my breasts. "Your tits have swollen up."

Not by much. They're not much bigger than they've always been. My nipples are a hell of a lot more sensitive now. He bites them when he's fucking me and I feel it instantly in my core. "They're still small."

"They're perfect." He plants a kiss on the side of my breasts. "Are you ready for round two?"

Round one lasted more than an hour. I was hungry for his cock when I got to his place, so I took him right inside the door. I pushed his jeans down along with his boxers and sucked him without abandon.

I almost got off myself just from the sounds he was making and the way he pulled my hair. He wasn't gentle when he came down my throat, heated words hissed from his lips and by the time he pulled me to my feet, I was wetter than I'd ever been.

He didn't waste any of it. He took me to bed, stripped me and ate my pussy until I rocked against his mouth. I could smell my arousal on his beard when he finally stopped the lashings and climbed on top of me.

"I love being pregnant." I push up so I can kiss him. "I like that we don't have to use a condom anymore."

We had a brief discussion after I found out I was pregnant about risk. I'd been tested in the hospital during the blood screen they ran after I was admitted. He was tested right before we met. It was a conversation that seemed unnecessary yet important to us both.

"That first night when I sank my cock into you without a condom, I thought I'd died," he repeats the words he's said at least a dozen times since I was in the hospital. "You can't possibly understand what it feels like, Sophia."

"I do." I wink at him. "I feel the same things you do."

"You can't." He grabs hold of his erection. "You feel what you feel and I feel this being gripped by you."

"You need to calm down or your penis is going to explode." I look down. "I can jack you off."

"You can talk dirty to me all day but I'm going to fuck you."

"Now?"

He slides his cock over my core, parting the seams of my pussy with the crown. "Now and then again tomorrow morning and then…"

"I get the picture." I moan as he slides the tip in. "Be gentle. Everything feels so sensitive right now."

"I'll be as gentle as I can be, but a man only has so much willpower when he's fucking the love of his life."

Chapter 37

Nicholas

"A book?" I straddle her. We fucked and then not two minutes later she whispered in my ear that she's considering an offer for a book deal from my publisher. "You're not serious?"

She pushes against my chest, a motion meant to urge me to roll to my side. I do. I prop my head up on one hand and stare down at her.

Jesus, she's beautiful. Her hair is a mess, her lips swollen from my teeth and tongue. She looks well fucked and loved.

"I haven't given them an answer." Her eyes take on a warm gleam. "I was honored that they even approached me. I'm a fashion designer, not a writer."

That's a lie. She's been writing to our baby in a journal. It's something she picked up from Cadence, although she hasn't yet told her best friend we're expecting. I've read her words and fuck me; they're filled with everything my heart wants to say.

She encouraged me to fill in pages of the journal with my own words, but I can't. I tried. I can write the hell out of a novel about murder and intrigue but I can't lay down a sentence for the child I can't wait to meet.

"When did they make the offer?" I'm curious. I've been on a book tour the last two weeks. I dialed it back after what happened to Sophia, but I've spent more than a few hours with my contact from the publishing house. He hasn't said a word about this although that's not surprising. I doubt like hell Sophia was offered a deal from the same imprint as my books.

"Yesterday." She blinks. "I told them I needed to talk to the man I love."

I'm glad. I would have been pissed if she would have given them an answer without my input. This is my wheelhouse. I'm the expert in this arena.

"I take it they want you to write about what happened with Franco?"

A smile ghosts her mouth. "That's the conclusion anyone would jump to in a situation like this."

"That's not an answer, Sophia." I rub my hand over her bare stomach. "What's the book about?"

"Love."

I press my hand to her breast. "Love? As in your love for me?"

She nods. "I might have done something right after we met."

I quirk both brows. "What might you have done?"

"This is embarrassing." She shields her eyes with both hands. "I started a blog."

"You what?"

"I started a blog about falling in love." She peeks out from between her splayed fingers. "All these women had these dating blogs and I'd read them. They were filled with so much doom and gloom."

"So you wanted to rewrite their stories?" I ask, mild confusion etching my words.

"No." She drops her hands. "I wanted to write *my* story. It was cathartic and helpful, and every night after I worked on my designs, I'd log on and write a post about that day.

"About us that day?"

"Sometimes." Her gaze drops to her stomach. "The blog has two parts. Past and present."

"Your past relationships and your present one?" I tap my forehead. "I think I'm catching on."

"The past was mostly about growing up and the dreams I had about falling in love. That's my past. The experiences I had pre-him."

"Him? Me?"

"Yes." She smiles. "My present is our story now. I've written about my heart on that blog. Finding you, loving you, discovering forever."

"You'll show it to me?"

"It was meant for only you." She reaches to the side table to grab her phone. "I was going to show it to you on our wedding night. I thought it was set to private, but I was wrong. A woman posted excerpts of it on her Pinterest account."

"Seriously?" His grin flashes.

"She linked back to my blog and traffic went through the roof. I've made it private since the publisher contacted me. They don't know it's me, by the way. I've never used my real name on the blog, or your name."

My eyes scan her phone's screen and the simple pink blog filled with words written from her heart. "They want to publish the content of this blog?"

"They do." She laughs. "When they sent me an email through the blog they said it was inspirational and a testament to a modern love story."

Our love story. "I'm going to read every word of this."

"For now, I want you to read the last post. I did that one earlier today."

I hand her the phone so that she can pull up the post. I start reading the moment she hands it back to me.

Him. He's the dream we all have at night when our heart is still empty. I wanted a forever love and always imagined when I found it that it would mirror what I saw in the kitchen of my parents' home when they were making Sunday dinners for the family. I thought I saw true love in my granddad's tears when he kissed my grandma's coffin before they lowered her into the ground.

Love with him is different.

It's grilled cheese sandwiches and piano sonnets.

It's broad shoulders, black hair, and an incredible mind.

It's trust, broken and then rebuilt.

It's tomorrow and a new life.

I'm going to ask him to marry me today. I don't have a ring. I have a heart. I gave it to him months ago and it's his forever.

P.S. I think he'll say yes.

"Yes," I whisper as I drop the phone on the bed between us. "Yes, Sophia. I will marry you."

Epilogue

Six Months Later

Sophia

"You're staring at your wedding ring again, Sophia."

I don't turn to look at him even though he's naked. "I love my ring, Nicholas. I don't think you could have picked a more perfect ring."

It's true. It's simple but elegant. It's a thin band of diamonds that represents our eternity. It's the only ring I can wear right now. I'm less than a month away from giving birth to our daughter. My oval cut diamond engagement ring is in the safe here in our new apartment, right next to a flash drive that contains every post from my blog.

I turned the publisher down. The posts were meant for my husband and even before he read them all, I knew that there would ever only be one author in our family. He's riding high on the success of *Action's Cause*.

"Gabriel told me that Ella Kara was just picked up by a big chain store in London."

I love how invested he is in my work. He was there when the collection launched and he held my hand as I navigated the many interviews and podcasts that followed. He coached me on how to handle the inevitable questions about the ordeal I went through with Elroy. I don't discuss it anymore. There's no need. Elroy is happy and I spent two months seeing a therapist Liam recommended. It helped.

"I'll need to fly there in a few months." I open the calendar app on my phone. "Gabriel sent me an email about the trip but I haven't looked it over yet."

"I'll handle it." He tips his chin toward my phone. "Forward that to me and I'll make all the arrangements. It will be Winter's first trip abroad."

Winter.

When we met.

When we fell in love and now, the name of our daughter.

Winter Rose Wolf.

"Maybe we can go to Paris too?" I shoot a pointed glance at his body. "I want to make love to my husband there."

"We'll bring your parents with us and get them a room on another floor." He laughs. "It will be a honeymoon for us and bonding time for them with Winter Rose."

"I can't wait." I clap my hands together. "I'm hungry. I should make something to eat."

"After what you just did for me, the least I can do is cook dinner for you."

Before his shower, I'd taken him in my mouth. I stroked my tongue along every ridge and vein of his cock. I lapped at the wide crown until he came hard and fast, the moan that escaped him sent shivers through my body.

"That's a deal."

"Then we'll take off for your surprise baby shower." He pulls on a pair of black boxers. "You're going to act surprised, Sophia."

"I will." I have to. Cadence went to a lot of trouble to plan this. She started the day I told her I was pregnant. I did it the day after she gave birth to Firi. He's a beautiful boy with a full head of blonde hair and brilliant blue eyes.

Den and I have joked since that Firi and Kara Foster will get married one day. I held her in my arms last week, a prelude to my own baby who I'll meet in just a few weeks.

"Put your hand here, Nicholas." I reach out for him. "She's dancing again."

He rushes to my side and drops to his knees. His hand darts to my belly. "I feel it. I feel my girl."

"She's the luckiest girl in the world."

"To have you as a mom," he interrupts me before he presses his lips to my skin. "I love you, Winter Rose. You, your mommy and I are going to have the most incredible adventure together."

"We will." I stroke his hair with my hand. "It's only going to get better from here."

Preview of Troublemaker

Crew

There are certain luxuries afforded a man when he owns a club in Manhattan. He can drink the best scotch in the world and expense that shit. He can pick a different woman every night of the week and he can sit on his ass and watch one of his best friends get hit on by some schmuck in a suit that's two sizes too big or he can do something about it.

I've had my fill of scotch tonight and the woman I was with last night is waiting for me back at her place. I can't leave my club, Veil East, yet. That's because, Adley York, one of my closest friends is about to go home with a professional baseball player with a reputation for hitting it out of the park.

It shouldn't matter to me if another man is stellar in bed. I don't compare myself to anyone. I've never had a complaint in all the years I've been active on the Manhattan social scene. I've fucked more women than Trey Hale, but by the look of what's happening on the dance floor, he's about to take Adley home to screw her.

That is not happening on my watch.

I can't have her because there are women that you friend and women that you fuck. Adley falls squarely in the first category although my traitorous cock wants her in the second. It can't happen. If I take that petite blond to bed, I'll lose her and the hole that would leave in my life is something I don't have the fucking emotional maturity to deal with.

"Adley," I call out her name over the booming beat that radiates off the walls. Why the hell did I have a state of the art sound system installed in this place? "Hey, Ad."

By the grace of God, she notices me pointing at her. She tosses me a wave and a wiggle of her ass before she grabs hold of the star pitcher's shoulders. I swear to fuck if she climbs up on that right now, I'll haul her off the floor over my shoulder.

I motion for her to come toward me and she flips me the bird.

I slam my now empty tumbler on the bar and stalk toward her.

"I need to talk to you." I stand next to her. "It's important, Adley."

"It can wait, Crew." Her pretty face flushes. "I'm a little busy right now."

She's a little drunk right now. I see it in her eyes and her hips. She's aching for some and if anyone is going to give it to her, it'll be me.

No. I fucking can't. Those perfect tits and that curvy ass are off-limits.

"I'm going to drop you off at your apartment." I take a quick look around. The club is running smoothly tonight. We're at full capacity. I don't need to be here to benefit from this. "Grab your stuff and let's go."

"Why would l do that?" Her eyes rake my six-foot –three, two-hundred-pound frame. "You're not as fun as Trey is."

Trey has nothing on me. I'm taller, richer, and a hell of a lot better looking than he is. I own a mirror. Dark hair, green eyes and a smile that has never failed me to date are what I see every morning.

"You've had too much to drink, Ad."

"Maybe you haven't had enough." She pokes her finger into my chest. "You work out."

Like a madman, every morning at five a.m. before the city wakes up. "We're leaving."

"What if I want to go with him?"

"Pick another night to make that happen." I direct that statement to Hale. "She's not going anywhere with you tonight."

"Who are you? Her husband?"

Adley laughs so hard she bends over revealing a perfect bird's eye view of the top of her round breasts. I swear to all things sacred, I'll look away, but I don't.

"I'm her friend. I own the club." I push a hand at him. "Crew Benton."

"You're Benton?" He steps closer and studies my face, his hand eagerly shaking mine. "Your reputation precedes you, man."

I have no idea what the fuck that means, so I steer him to a place I'll know he'll go. "Your drinks are on the house for the rest of the night. Tell Penny at the bar, Crew's taking the tab."

"No shit?"

"No shit," I repeat back. "It's a limited time offer so..."

"Understood." He doesn't give Adley another look before he heads for the bar.

"That was a cock-block, a totally intentional cock-block." She frowns. "You ruined my night. Now, what am I supposed to do?"

I eye her up. Small black dress, hair so messed up that she looks like she just fucked in the back of a beat-up pickup truck and a mouth that was made for sin. "Come to my place, Adley. I want you to come home with me."

Coming soon

THANK YOU

Thank you for purchasing my book. I can't even begin to put to words what it means to me. If you enjoyed it, please remember to write a review for it. Let me know your thoughts! I want to keep my readers happy.

For more information on new series and standalones, please visit my website, www.deborahbladon.com. There are book trailers and other goodies to check out.

If you want to chat with me personally, please LIKE my page on Facebook. I love connecting with all of my readers because without you, none of this would be possible.
www.facebook.com/authordeborahbladon

Thank you, for everything.

ABOUT THE AUTHOR

Deborah Bladon has never read a romance hero she didn't like. Her love for romance novels began when she was old enough to board the bus, library card in hand to check out the newest Harlequin paperbacks. She's a Canadian by heart, and by passport, but you can often spot her in New York City sipping a latte and looking for inspiration for her next story. Manhattan is definitely her second home.

She cherishes her family and believes that each day is a gift for writing, for reading, and for loving.